A CYBERPUNK SUPERHERO NOVEL

RONIN BORN

BY PERCIVAL CONSTANTINE

Other series by Percival Constantine

LUTHER CROSS

This dangerously handsome, effortlessly stylish half-demon is Chicago's foremost paranormal investigator. With magical aptitude and specialized weapons, Luther Cross will handle your supernatural problems… for the right price.

MORNINGSTAR

God is dead but the Devil is real. And now he's on Earth. Everything you know about Lucifer and his rebellion from Heaven is a lie. Now, free of his responsibilities, Lucifer has come to walk amongst humanity to discover just what exactly it means to be free.

THE MYTH HUNTER

All the legends of the world have some element of truth to them. And to track down those legends, there are the myth hunters. Some, like Elisa Hill, are explorers, trying to learn more about the world. And some are soldiers of fortune, whose only goal is profit and exploitation, no matter the risk.

INFERNUM

A shadowy, globe-spanning network of operatives run by the mysterious power broker known as Dante. They hold allegiance to no one, existing as rogues on the fringes of society. No matter the job, Infernum has an operative to execute it—provided you have the means to pay for it!

VANGUARD

The world has changed. A mysterious event altered the genetic structure of humanity, granting a small percentage of the population superhuman powers. A small team of these specials has been formed to deal with potential threats. Paragon—telekinetic powerhouse; Zenith—hyper-intelligent automaton; Shift—shape-changing teenager; Wraith—teleporting shadow warrior; Sharkskin—human/shark hybrid. Led by the armored Gunsmith, they are Vanguard!

Visit PercivalConstantine.com for an up-to-date list of titles!

CHAPTER 1

Erika Kuroki grunted as her back hit the padded wall. She fell on the ground and looked up through strands of black hair at the man who threw her. He wore a black training *gi*, same as hers. He was in his mid-thirties, just a little bit older than she was, and he sported a thin beard.

"Get up," he said.

Erika got to her feet and moved into a fighting stance. She felt a charge go through her body as the implants adjusted. The cybernetic implants fed her diagnostic information about her target, advising her on the best course of action. Erika ignored it, choosing to rely on her own instincts instead.

Hiro grinned at her and she came at him. She sprung, extending her leg out in a kick as she flew through the air. Hiro was ready for her and grabbed the leg, twisting and slamming her back onto the padded floor. He kept her pinned there and Erika struggled to move.

"Cybernetic enhancements don't mean a whole lot

when your opponent has them, too," said Hiro, one arm braced against her chest, the other hand still holding her leg.

Erika swung her free leg up and jammed her knee against the side of Hiro's head. She stunned him and managed to pull herself from his grip. She got to her feet and delivered another blow to his chest, knocking him on his back.

"Good thing I learned to fight long before I got these enhancements," said Erika. "Now are you ready to surrender?"

He stood and scoffed. "Don't make me laugh. I could keep this up all day."

She came at him again, but every punch she tried to land, he was able to counter. Every kick, he blocked. As more of her attacks failed, her frustration only grew. And that frustration only drove her to push herself harder, letting anger start to cloud her judgment.

Hiro's greatest skill wasn't his fighting ability, nor how adept he was with his enhancements. He had a keen insight into people and knew just how to push their buttons. It was a talent that gave him the upper edge in combat, which was why even in his short career he'd gained a reputation as one of the Tokkei's top agents.

His hands moved like a blur, mostly content with playing defense. Erika kept trying to strike faster and harder, but no matter how fast or how hard she hit, Hiro was there with a deflection. And then, just when she thought she could keep it up no longer, he dropped to the floor and swept her legs with his own. She was knocked off her feet and once again he was on top of her. This time, though, he pinned her down with his entire body, immobilizing her. She tried to struggle for a few moments, but once she realized it was useless, she relaxed her body and went limp.

Hiro climbed off her and offered his hand. Erika gripped it with her own and he pulled her up. She sighed and walked over to the corner of the room where a water bottle and towel waited. Erika wiped the sweat from her face and squired the water into her mouth, then sighed.

"Nice work," he said.

"Don't patronize me."

"I'm serious," said Hiro. "You've taken to the implants remarkably well. That's not something easily achieved."

"I'm still not used to them. The eye thing especially feels weird."

That "eye thing" she referred to was the augmented-reality heads-up display or AR-HUD. Her implants could display a variety of information over her retina, anything from GPS directions to text messages. Anyone with AR-HUD-enabled implants was essentially a walking smartphone.

He chuckled and wiped his face with his own towel. "It takes some getting used to, I'll grant you that. But at the rate you're going, I wouldn't be surprised if you got sent on your first mission soon."

Erika blinked. "Already? It's only been about a month."

"If you weren't Tokkei quality, you wouldn't be here in the first place. The training is about helping you familiarize yourself with your implants. But once that's done, it's off to the races."

"And are most ready that quickly?"

Hiro smirked. "I see what you're trying to do. And it's not going to work."

He turned and walked for the exit. Erika jogged a bit to

catch up to his side. She moved into step next to him, but he didn't glance to acknowledge her, just drank more water and continued moving down the corridor.

"What's not going to work?" she asked.

He scoffed. "You want me to tell you, 'Oh Kuroki, you're amazing. No one has ever advanced as fast as you. Truly you're a gift to the whole nation.'"

"Just because you won't say it doesn't mean it isn't true."

He chuckled, then stopped and turned to face her. "Listen, I know you were hot shit in the Jietai. But this is a whole different game you're playing now. You can't afford to get cocky."

"It's not cocky if it's the truth."

He shook his head. "I guess hafu don't understand the concept of modesty."

Erika bristled at the sound of that word. She had risen through the Jietai and earned enough commodations in the war to earn an officer rank. She even took her mother's surname. After everything, she'd hoped she'd earned the right to be judged by her actions and not her ancestry.

"I understand it just fine," she said, her tone now flat. "I have to clean up and then return home. Send me a message once the next session is scheduled."

She turned and continued down the corridor, leaving Hiro behind her. Part of her felt ashamed as she continued on her path to the women's bathing facilities. Since she was promoted to the Tokkei, Hiro had been very kind to her. In fact, this was the first time he even said anything about her heritage. He'd known from the start, of course.

All children were given a DNA scan at birth. It was a mark that stayed with them for the rest of their lives. Even though Erika was born here and had never known any home besides Japan, in the eyes of the government, birthright citizenship was only granted to full-blooded Japanese. *Hafu*, or those of mixed-race Japanese descent, could obtain citizenship, but only through government service, usually military.

Erika pushed those thoughts from her mind. A bath would help her clear her head and focus on what was more important.

Or so she had hoped. But after showering off, she climbed into the hot communal bath and sat against the edge of the large tub, the water level up to her neck. She raised her arm above the water's surface and turned it, examining it in the low light. Erika touched her fingers to her forearm, running them down the surface.

Her cybernetic implants were beneath the surface, completely invisible to the naked eye. Tokkei agents had to be able to move about freely and without notice—having visible cybernetic parts attached would obviously make that more difficult. She still found it strange. On the outside, she was the same person she was in the Jietai. But on the inside, she was different. Better.

A few other women had entered the bathing area. They were Tokkei as well—this level of the building was reserved for agents and personnel. And though they looked at Erika, they made no attempts to engage her in conversation.

The more things change… she thought to herself.

Erika got out of the bath and returned to the changing area. She dried herself off and dressed in clean clothes. There was nothing more to do here and she just wanted to get home and relax. It was clear she still had a long way to go to prove herself.

The Ministry of Defense was located in Shinjuku,

one of Tokyo's largest neighborhoods. Erika exited from the front entrance and walked down the steps of the tall building. It used to be a much smaller building in the days before the government revised the pacifist constitution. Now the Ministry of Defense was one of Japan's top budget priorities. And it showed as the reconstructed headquarters was a massive campus with one of the tallest buildings in Tokyo—if not the nation.

She walked down the steps leading from the main building. The main gate consisted of an energy barrier and included a genetic scanner. When someone attempted to pass through, their biometrics were instantly checked, down to their DNA. If one had clearance, the barrier may as well be invisible. But if not, the infiltrator would be instantly incapacitated and then arrested. Guards were present as well. They wore armor styled after the samurai of the Edo period, though it was much more advanced. The Tokkei had armor of their own they wore on certain missions. Similar to what these guards had, but more distinctive and more powerful.

Erika passed through the barrier without issue. The guards didn't even look at her, though she doubted she could tell if they did. Their helmet faceplates were styled much like the masks of old, in the form of demonic visages.

The train station was ten minutes away on foot. Erika was looking forward to getting home. She still couldn't help the feeling of unease. Becoming an officer in the Jietai and then earning an invitation to the Tokkei? It was more than she could have possibly wished for when she first enlisted. So why then, after all that hard work, did she still feel that something was missing? After all, in the eyes of the government, she'd finally earned her citizenship. That was something many born like her had wished for, but could never claim.

It was almost six in the evening, so the station was crowded with commuters trying to make it home. A sea of people dressed in suits and school uniforms moved almost as one down the steps and into the station below. Erika was about to join them, but her eye was caught by a man sitting near the entrance. He was shabbily dressed and from the look and smell, hadn't showered in days. There was a sign propped up against his leg, with the word "help" scrawled on it in English. His blue eyes made contact with hers and she just stared at the derelict for a few moments.

The moment ended once he was pulled to his feet by uniformed police officers. They started shouting at him in Japanese. Erika was too far away to make out everything they said, but the general gist of it seemed to be that he'd been a nuisance in this area for some time. The cops seemed to be out of warnings and dragged him off, with him protesting in a mix of English and broken Japanese.

"Disgusting, isn't it?"

Erika was surprised she didn't notice the person next to her. She looked over and saw a woman about the same age as her, wearing the blouse, vest, and skirt of a government employee.

"I'm sorry, I didn't hear what you said."

The woman looked at Erika, then back to where the man was. "I said disgusting. That bum was hanging around here every single day for the past week. I tried to tell the police, but all they did was give him warnings at first. They finally got rid of him." Her face bore a visage of revulsion. "Those people. We invited them in and now they've become a drain on society. Maybe we shouldn't have even bothered.

Just send them all back where they came from."

"No, maybe not…" muttered Erika.

She wondered what would become of that man. Would he be taken to a shelter or did he have family? She decided she didn't really want to know and instead, joined the crowd moving down into the station. Maybe the woman was right, maybe things would be better if all of them were rounded up and sent back to their own countries.

Erika became lost within the crowd of commuters, just another face almost indistinguishable from the rest. She waited patiently for the train with the others, and when it did finally arrive, she would ride it in silence to her apartment.

CHAPTER 2

Hiro Yoshida marched down the corridor, wearing a military dress uniform. When he reached the door, he knocked and a voice beckoned for him to enter. Hiro opened the door and stepped inside, walking up to a large desk. A cloud of smoke hung in the air and behind the desk sat an older man in a uniform with a graying mustache and a receding hairline. The cloud came from the cigarette clasped in his fingers. A holo-screen projected from the desk and that's where his concentration was focused.

"Hiro Yoshida, Tokkei Agent," said Hiro before bowing deeply. "It is an honor to be summoned before you, General Hojo."

Hojo's eyes moved from the screen and took in Hiro. He waved his hand and the holo-screen vanished. Hojo leaned back in his chair and took a drag on his cigarette. "Thank you for coming to see me, Agent Yoshida. I'm interested in seeing how your evaluations have been coming along."

"Very well, sir," said Hiro. "Have you received my reports?"

Hojo gestured to the now-vanished holo-screen. "I was just reading them actually."

"Is there anything specific you would like me to comment on, sir?"

"Give me your general impressions of the new recruits."

"They're quite good, which is to be expected. Tokkei recruiters have extremely high standards, so it's very rare to see any surprises."

"Any stand-outs?"

"A few. Masao Ishiyama has an excellent command of hand-to-hand combat. And Sayuri Tanaka seems to have the makings of an infiltration expert. And of course, there's Erika Kuroki."

"Yes, about that one…"

Hojo waved his hand up and the holo-screen appeared again. He touched the screen and entered the first few characters of Erika's name, then selected from the suggested options. Her main file opened up on the screen and a few additional screens appeared around the desk, each one on a different category—military history, family registry, education, medical records, as well as several photos and videos of her over the years.

"She's a curious addition," said Hojo. "Given her family's background."

"Yes, I'm aware," said Hiro.

"Were you also aware that her father was once labeled as a potential insurgent?"

"Of course, I make it a point to thoroughly review the history of every recruit assigned to me."

"And you found nothing unusual about this little fact?"

"Not particularly, no," said Hiro. "Naturally when I first saw it, I was suspicious, so I opened an investigation."

"And what did you learn?"

"Nothing that would justify denying Agent Kuroki a position."

"You'll have to explain that, son."

"She was born in Osaka, but her parents divorced before she reached the age of ten. As you'd expect, the mother took the child back to her family home in Shizuoka while the father remained in Osaka, where he held a position at a university. Erika never had any contact with her father again after that."

"And her name?"

"When her parents married, the mother kept her own name. Her mother's dead so I couldn't get an answer from her directly, but I did speak to a relative who said Erika's parents decided the mother would keep her own name to make life easier for any potential children."

"Hmph." Hojo huffed at that and took another drag on the cigarette. "I'm not comfortable involving this one in the Tokkei. The things we're called on…someone like her might find it distasteful."

"With all due respect, sir, may I speak freely?"

"Go on."

"Erika Kuroki has an exemplary record, even before she joined the Jietai. She's shown nothing but the highest degree of patriotism. She's intelligent, highly skilled, and her adjustment period with the implants is far shorter than the average for new inductions. I was just training with her earlier today and I feel she has the makings of a model agent."

Hojo's eyes moved between the various holo-screens

containing Erika's records. He rubbed his chin in thought with one hand, the other stamping out what was left of the cigarette in a half-filled ashtray. Again his eyes met Hiro's, who bowed his head and looked down at the floor. With another wave of his hand, Hojo dismissed the screens. He reached for a small, flat object on the corner of his desk and held it up for Hiro.

"A new assignment's come down the pipeline. This was forwarded from Tokyo Met," he said, referring to the Tokyo Metropolitan Police.

Hiro accepted the small diskette and held it in the palm of his hand. The implants in there read the data off the diskette and he was now seeing it as a holo-screen in front of his face. The image was of an older man in a suit with no tie, flanked by bigger, younger men who wore sunglasses.

"Is that who I think it is?" asked Hiro.

"Junichi Kitano himself," said Hojo. "They've gotten a break in the search for his clinics. We've taken over juris-diction of the case and I want you on the team that goes to bring him in."

"Is the Tokkei really necessary to bring in a yakuza thug?" asked Hiro.

"His black market clinics not only handle genetic counterfeiting, but they also perform illegal cybernetic im-plantations. Those men you see in the surveillance photos? They're all sporting implants. This is more than the Met can handle."

"I understand," said Hiro. "Are you giving me full license to choose my team?"

Hojo raised an eyebrow. "That depends, who are you thinking of?"

"I think this would be a good time for those recruits

I mentioned to see some action in the field. Ishiyama, Tanaka, and Kuroki.”

“I have no objections to Ishiyama or Tanaka, but Kuroki…”

“General, I beg you to reconsider. Kuroki simply needs an opportunity to prove herself, and I believe once you see her in action, you’ll agree that she belongs in the Tokkei.”

Hojo sighed and shook his head. “Fine, I’ll allow it. But I’m also putting you on notice here, Yoshida—if this doesn’t work out, you’ll be the one who takes the blame for it.”

“It’s a responsibility I humbly accept, General.” Hiro bowed. “When should we begin?”

“Review the data and present me with a proposal for the operation by tonight. If it’s approved, you brief your team and move tomorrow.”

“Understood, sir.”

“Good, now go. You’ve got a lot of work to get to,” said Hojo.

CHAPTER 3

Erika went up to the turnstile at the train station entrance. She pushed her thumb against the touchpad and the small doors opened to allow her entry. Before, people would carry around wallets with their identification, credit cards, and cash. Then all that became consolidated in their phones. Now, those phones had become wearable devices—watches, glasses, earbuds. Some underwent operations for cybernetic implants, but they were very expensive and even then, the only implants legal for civillians were the kind that essentially turned a person into a walking smartphone. With those implants, bank accounts and credit cards could be linked together, allowing to pay for services with the touch of a finger.

Of course, as a Tokkei agent, Erika's implants were far more sophisticated and could do a lot beyond handling her train fare.

There was never a time when Shinjuku Station wasn't crowded. But even still, it was less than usual at this time of morning. She didn't manage to grab a seat on the train, but at least she wasn't shoved up against anyone. Erika passed the time during the twenty-minute commute by bringing up the day's newsfeed on her AR-HUD. Though calling it news was a bit much as it read more like celebrity gossip. Still, it provided something to distract her until the automated voice announced Erika's stop.

When she reached the Ministry of Defense, she saw the armored guards flanking the entrance as usual. She walked through the barrier, the scanner detecting her genetic markers and allowing her access without harm. As soon as she entered the lobby, she was surprised to see Hiro was waiting for her.

"'Morning," he said.

"Sorry to keep you waiting."

He waved it off. "Don't worry about it. Though the others are here, so we should go downstairs for the briefing."

Erika nodded and Hiro led her to the elevator. As they walked through the doors, the biometric scanners did their work and confirmed their identities and clearance.

"Sub-level B," said Hiro.

"Access granted," came the elevator's response.

"What's so important that I had to get out of bed before dawn?" asked Erika.

"You'll find out at the briefing," said Hiro, then didn't say another word. Erika followed his lead and remained quiet.

The elevator reached its destination and Hiro led her down a series of corridors until they came to a pair of glass doors. They opened as soon as Hiro stopped in front of them. Inside was a round table and holographic monitors along the wall displaying surveillance feeds from across the city. Sitting at the table were two other agents. One was a woman about the same age as Erika with long hair. The other was a man with broad shoulders and a shaved head. His face looked like it had been chiseled from stone.

"Not sure if you've had a chance to get acquainted yet," said Hiro. "Ishiyama, Tanaka, this is Kuroki. She'll also be joining us on this mission."

The two agents stood and bowed and Erika did the same. She'd met Masao Ishiyama, the big guy, before. At one point, they both served on the same base when they were enrolled in the Jietai. But Erika had been more concerned with proving herself to her superiors than with making friends, so she tended to keep to herself. She did remember he had a reputation as a good fighter, though she hadn't really had the opportunity to see him in action. Sayuri Tanaka was a name Erika had heard before, but other than some whispers of her exploits, she was mostly a ghost. Erika supposed that was what made her a perfect Tokkei candidate.

"Now that we're all here, let's begin the briefing."

Hiro took an empty seat at the table and motioned for Erika to do the same, while Both Masao and Sayuri returned to their own. Once everyone was seated, Hiro used his cybernetics to interface with the table's holographic projector. A 3D image appeared in front of them in the form of an older man with graying hair and dressed in a suit with no tie.

"For anyone who doesn't recognize him, this is Junichi Kitano," said Hiro. "Runs a small yakuza clan that's affiliated with the Yamazaki-gumi. He's reclusive and very slippery, but the Met finally got a break and we have a location on him. He's our target."

"Excuse me, sir," said Masao. "But why send the Tokkei after this guy?"

"That's the exact same question I had," said Hiro. "You see, like all these thugs, Kitano is involved in a bit of everything. Gambling, prostitution, drugs. But his primary stock and trade is black market cybernetics. And he's given his men free upgrades."

"That's one of the reasons he's stayed invisible," said Sayuri. "Anyone starts sniffing around his trail, his men take care of them with lethal precision."

"Exactly right, Tanaka," said Hiro. "Even if we did send a Special Assault Team in, there's no guarantee they could succeed. Plus, the Minister wants to keep this quiet and that's hard to do when SAT's involved."

"What's the plan?" asked Sayuri.

"Four-man team, just us. With our equipment, this should be a fairly simple op. We go in, we take out Kitano's men, capture him, and download his files. All without causing too much of a scene. And to help you with that…"

Hiro reached under the table and picked up a metal case. He set it on the surface and opened it, turning the case so the three agents could see the contents. There were three devices inside that looked like bulky smartwatches.

"The devices are containers for nanomachines," said Hiro and he held up his right arm to reveal that he wore one, too.

Nanomachines suddenly spread out from the watch, covering him from head to toe in black and red armor, including a helmet and mask. The design of the look was inspired by the samurai of old, though it appeared to have a modern twist. A moment later, the nanobots retreated back into the device.

"The armor is cutting edge. Provides you with a large degree of invulnerability, and interfaces with your existing implants to increase your speed, strength, and reflexes even more."

"Weapons?" asked Erika.

"It can generate an energized katana, with both lethal and non-lethal settings. Also capable of firing off an energy burst from the sword," said Hiro.

"No training before taking these out into the field?" asked Erika. "You sure that's a good idea?"

Masao laughed. "Come on, don't tell me the big war hero's getting cold feet."

Erika shook her head. "No, it's not that. I just—"

Sayuri interjected. "Kuroki has a point, sir."

"She does at that," said Hiro. "I do wish we had longer, but time is a factor here and the training you've already gone through should be sufficient. There are more advanced features with the suit, which you'll learn about in time. Right now, we need to get moving. So put these on."

Each of them took one of the devices from the case and fastened them to their wrists. Erika looked at the display and saw a red progress wheel. As soon as the wheel filled, it changed to green and "INTERFACE COMPLETE" appeared.

"First time you put it on, the nanobots key to your cybernetic implants. Ensures that only you can use the suit. Even if those containers are put on by someone else, they won't be able to use the nanobots. And your implants can track the container anywhere it goes," said Hiro. "Go on, try the suits out."

"How do they work?" asked Masao.

"The cybernetic link might take some time to get used

to, so for now just tap the display," said Hiro. "As you get more comfortable, you and the suit will have a symbiotic relationship.

Erika tapped the display twice. She heard a sound that was similar to a metallic scraping noise and she felt the microscopic machines crawl over her body. The sensation nearly spooked her—as if she'd been swarmed by thousands of insects. But once the suit was in place, she could relax. Diagnostic information was projected against her retina on a AR-HUD. She held up her hand and examined the armor.

Despite that initial strange sensation, now that the suit was active, it felt surprisingly comfortable. Based on the appearance, she would have thought that it would be heavy or bulky. Or at the very least uncomfortable. But she found no restrictions whatsoever in her movements. She tested out some quick punches and kicks and found it was incredibly easy to move. When she finally broke out of her own world, she looked at her teammates and saw that Masao and Sayuri had both armored up and were testing out the movements for themselves.

"Very good," said Hiro. "But keep your suits concealed until you need them. We don't want to spook any of the normies."

"And where are we going?" asked Erika as she tapped the display again, sending the nanobots back into their container.

"Yoshiwara. Which is exactly where you'd expect to find a yakuza thug involved in human trafficking," said Hiro.

"And how do we get there?" asked Sayuri.

"Same way everyone else does—we take the train."

Masao grumbled. "Aww, c'mon. I thought the Tokkei

was supposed to be the elitest of the elite. And you're sayin' we gotta ride public transport with the rest of the rubes?"

"Don't quite understand the concept of 'low-profile,' do you?" asked Erika with a chuckle. Sayuri snickered along with her.

"Hey, just look at me." Masao gestured to his large frame. "Nothin' about me is low-profile."

"Then you'll work nicely as a human shield," said Hiro and the others laughed. "Jokes aside, we want to try to keep this as quiet as possible. Stealth tactics. Stay in contact with each other at all times and don't make too much noise. The suits will help you eliminate the targets quickly and cleanly."

"Do we have any idea what kind of place we're walking into?" asked Erika.

"As a matter of fact, yes." Hiro turned to the table and a holographic projection of a building approximately five stories tall appeared, with a pagoda-style roof. There was a heavy emphasis on red and gold in the design, very much in the classic style of the Yoshiwara of old. "We believe this is the house Kitano runs. On the surface it's a casino, but those upper floors are rooms for…let's say 'special arrangements' between the customers and waitresses."

The prostitution loophole. On paper, prostitution was illegal. But in practice, they weren't explicitly providing sex—just company. And if sex happened to occur, that was a separate arrangement between the two parties. It was a loophole that dictated the way the system operated ever since prostitution was first outlawed after the Second World War.

"Question, boss: Would it be okay if—?"

"No," said Hiro, cutting off Masao before he could ask

the question. "One of the reasons we're going in so early is because the number of people at the compound will be far fewer. Far easier to get the files and find Kitano."

"And you're sure he's there?" asked Erika.

Hiro nodded. "Our intel says that he has his own apartment that takes up the entire top floor of the building. That's likely where he'll be, no doubt with guards watching over him. Ishiyama and Tanaka, that'll be your task. Take down his guards and capture him."

"And us?" asked Erika.

"Sub-levels are where we believe the cybernetics clinic is operated. That should be where we can find the data we need," said Hiro. "We split up when we get to Yoshiwara. Ishiyama and Tanaka will find points of entry from up top, while Kuroki and I find ones from below. Here are some suggestions."

The color drained from the holographic model and certain areas were highlighted to illustrate potential entry points.

"Ultimately you'll decide your own path based on the situation," said Hiro. "Unless there are any other questions…?"

The three newly minted Tokkei agents exchanged glances, but each one shook their head. Hiro nodded in approval.

"Very good. In that case, it's time to head out. We've got a train to catch."

CHAPTER 4

Yoshiwara had a long and sordid history. It began as a red-light district during the Edo era when the Tokugawa shogunate enacted a law that confined prostitution to designated areas. To this day, little had changed. Though the flesh trade that brothels once openly advertised was now spoken of in euphemisms.

It was just after eight in the morning by the time Erika and Hiro began walking the streets of Yoshiwara, and it was practically a ghost town. Though some shops operated during the day, most of them were only nighttime affairs, using the façade of being simple bars or restaurants. The ones that were open while the sun was up advertised themselves as massage parlors.

There were some drunks stumbling around. The latest bars closed at six in the morning, and some patrons lingered around after. Erika and Hiro ignored them as they moved through the district. At night, these shops and streets were lit up with bright lights and there would be girls standing out in front, clothed in skimpy dresses and trying to lure in customers. But under the harsh sunlight, it took on a much more depressing appearance.

Hiro held up his hand to stop Erika when they came to an intersection. He pointed down the street to the right, just around the corner from where they stood. Erika saw the same building from the briefing, with its pagoda roof and red and gold exterior.

"You get anything?" she asked.

"Can't get a full read, would have to suit up to access the complete scanner," said Hiro, focusing his gaze at the building. "And don't want to do that out on the street."

"Tanaka, you copy?" Erika kept her voice barely above a whisper. The implants could transmit her voice easily to the other team regardless of how soft it was.

"Copy." Sayuri's voice rang inside Erika and Hiro's heads.

"You see an entrance for yourselves?" she asked.

"The rooms have small balconies, Ishiyama and I will each enter through one. How about you two?"

"Still trying to find the best way in," said Hiro. "Be careful."

"Understood. We're about to move, so I'm going to go radio silent. Tanaka out."

"Just us now," said Erika.

"Walk down the street, see if you see anything in front," said Hiro. "I'm going to circle around back, try and check for other entrances."

Erika nodded and turned the corner on her own. Her heart started to speed up, and she wasn't sure if she was nervous or excited. But she kept moving down the street, trying to calm herself so she didn't get her adrenaline up too soon. A man stood outside the building's front entrance, lighting up a cigarette. He wore a suit and had sunglasses on, and he was about the same size as Ishiyama.

But as she approacned, he made eye contact with her. Erika turned from his gaze and passed in front of the entrance. She could still feel his eyes on her. A glance over her shoulder confirmed he was indeed still watching her.

"There's a guard in front, he's watching me," she whispered.

"Stay cool, just keep moving," came Hiro's reply.

"What's your status?"

"I'm at the back, it's also guarded. We might have to incapacitate them, but I'm a bit loathe to do it out in the open."

"What if we don't have to?" said Erika. "I think I have an idea."

"What sort of idea is that?"

"Just stay quiet and wait for my signal."

"Kuroki, don't do anything stupid, you hear me? Kuroki? Kuro—"

"Sorry, boss. I'm going silent now." Erika disabled her communicator and turned around. She still saw the guard staring at her, but now she stared back as she came closer to the entrance.

But just before she was about to walk up the stone steps to the front door, she turned away. She played up her uncertainty and paced back and forth a few times, the guard watching her each movement carefully.

"What are you doing?" he finally asked.

Erika feigned a gasp and snapped her head in his direction. She quickly turned away again and started to walk off to the side. The guard came down the steps and called after her.

"Hey!"

"I'm sorry!" she shouted back. "I…I probably shouldn't be here…"

"Why *are* you here?"

Erika stopped and turned back to him. She slowly approached him. "I…I lost my job. A friend of mine, she said I could probably find one here."

The man lowered his sunglasses, his eyes traveling up and down her body. His faced remained expressionless as he sized her up. He grabbed her chin and turned her head to each side, studying her facial features.

If you don't get your hands off me, I'm going to rip your balls off and shove them down your throat!

It took everything in her power *not* to vocalize that thought. But she knew she had to remain composed. She couldn't risk blowing the mission, so she had to play along and give the acting performance of her life. The guard released her face and sighed. She wasn't sure if that was a good sign or not.

"You know what kind of place this is? What kind of work you'd be doing?"

She looked down and nodded with a hint of shame. Erika wanted to sell her desperation. Might tug at what few heartstrings the guard had, if any. The guard continued to study her face, probably watching for any sign of her breaking character. He clearly wanted to be positive she was telling the truth.

"Where are you from?"

She looked up at him. "Shizuoka. I came to Tokyo last year for a job, but they've been cutting back."

"What kind of work did you do before?"

"Waitress."

"Hold on a minute."

He turned away and Erika watched as he tapped his smartwatch. He started speaking in a low voice. Erika's implants increased her hearing and she could make out what he was saying. Whoever he was talking to was a different story. But suffice to say, it seemed like her ploy worked and she kept her smile suppressed once he ended the call and turned back to her.

"Come on inside," he said. "There's someone you can talk to."

Erika nodded and followed him as he led her inside. The first floor was exactly as Hiro described. It was a fairly spacious casino with a large, circular bar in the center, though the restaurant was just as deserted as the streets of Yoshiwara. The guard closed and locked the door behind them.

"The boss is finishing up some things, so you can have a drink at the bar if you want. Once he's ready, he'll come down." The guard walked past her and towards the bar. "What's your poison?"

"Umm…maybe a cocktail," said Erika. "Say, do you mind if I use your bathroom?"

The guard was about to step behind the bar, but he sighed and motioned for her to follow. Erika caught up to him, walking behind him as he led her down a narrow corridor. While she followed, she tapped her device, and felt the nanobots crawling over her skin.

There were two open doorways with curtains. One had the symbol for man, and the other for woman. The nanites formed the *tsuka* or katana hilt in her hand. With nothing more than a thought, she activated the energy blade. It went right through the guard and he gasped just before collapsing on the ground.

Erika deactivated the sword and disengaged the armor, returning the nanobots to their container. She dragged him inside the women's bathroom and sat him up on one of the toilets. She closed the door and then returned to the corridor.

The energy blade was set to kill. Any post-mortem examination would conclude he died of a heart attack. She activated her communicator again. "Yoshida, you still alive?"

"Where the hell have you been? Do you have any idea how worried I was?"

"I'm in, come around by the front."

"What? How did you—"

"Just do it, I'll be waiting. Kuroki out."

Tanaka and Ishiyama still hadn't broken their silence, which meant they were still in the midst of going after Kitano. Either that, or they'd been captured. But all she could do was focus on the job at hand. Erika was careful as she moved from the bathroom corridor to the front of the casino, keeping a careful eye and monitoring her senses closely. She opened the front door, but saw no one.

"Yoshida, where are you? I'm at the fro—"

A figure dropped down in front of the door. Erika jumped back, instinctively moving into a defensive stance. She relaxed when she saw it was just Hiro. Erika sighed and stood up straight as he moved inside.

"Nearly gave me a heart attack," she said.

"Now you know how it feels," said Hiro. "Suit up, we'll need the full capabilities of our armor."

Erika tapped the container again and sighed as she felt the nanobots crawling over her body. Once the armor was in place, she looked at Hiro. "I hate that feeling."

"You get used to it," he replied. "Your armor's equipped with different scanning modes—x-ray, infrared, radio waves, etc. And right now, I'm scanning some strong electronic frequencies coming from below."

"You *did* say it was underground."

"Right, the question is how do we get there…" Hiro looked around the casino, slowly moving as he did, trying to locate the proper entry point. "Got it. Come with me."

A curtain blocked a doorway that had the kanji for staff only. They both went past the curtain and into the kitchen area. Hiro navigated through the kitchen easily, finding another door that led to a storeroom. Past the boxes, the storeroom had a trap door. Hiro knelt down and examined it closely, then sighed.

"Biometric lock," he said.

"Can you bypass it?" asked Erika.

"Guess we're about to find out…"

Hiro placed his hand on the scanning pad and it flashed red. But with contact, he could make a connection to the device's network. Erika held the sword tsuka in her hand and watched the storeroom entrance, waiting for anyone who might have come looking for the guard she'd killed.

"That's strange," said Hiro.

"What is it?" she asked.

"The security on this thing…it's military-grade."

"How'd someone like Kitano get his hands on something like that?"

"That's what we're going to find out. Because as good as his tech is…"

The pad flashed green and they heard the sound of locks disengaging. Hiro clapped once in victory.

"Hah! Mine's better."

The hatch opened automatically and revealed a staircase going down. Both of them entered, going into the basement. Everything was made of concrete and the darkness immediately activated the night-vision mode on their suits. Doors were off to each side of the corridor. Erika would look into them and see diagrams, charts, as well as cybernetic parts and surgical tools.

"Isn't this cozy," said Hiro.

"Who would trust cybernetic implants in a place like this?" asked Erika, noticing some bloodstains on the ground.

"People who have nothing to lose," said Hiro. "You'd be surprised just how powerful that sort of thing is."

She didn't even want to think about it.

"The signal's coming from here," said Hiro. He moved first and Erika followed until they came to a server room. He found the lights and as soon as they came on, the armor instantly returned to normal vision without any disorientation or harm to their eyes.

"This it?" asked Erika.

"Sure is," said Hiro. "Keep watch, I'll begin the download."

She nodded and went back from the corridor. But as she moved down the hall, her motion sensors picked up movement. Erika pushed her back up against the wall and gripped the sword hilt tightly.

They weren't alone down here.

CHAPTER 5

Masao Ishiyama was crouched on a rooftop just across from Kitano's Yoshiwara casino. Even though he and Sayuri were at a vantage point where no one from the street could look up and see them, he still felt exposed standing there in the morning.

"Right there." Sayuri pointed to the holographic model of the building. "Two balconies, one connected to Kitano's bedroom. You use it to enter his balcony, I'll take the other and eliminate any opposition."

"You seem pretty confident," said Masao. "Sure you can handle any guards yourself?"

"According to the readings I'm getting, seems most of them aren't in the rooms. Which makes sense. If anything, they'd expect potential threats to come in from the ground floor, not through the balconies. Seems to just be a few of them."

Sayuri looked up, as if something had distracted her. She turned her head to the side and Masao heard her say,

"Copy." Must have been a call from Hiro and Erika.

As Sayuri took the call, Masao just studied the balcony. His AR-HUD calculated the precise speed to run and the exact spot where he should jump from to cross the distance between the two buildings. This whole thing felt like a strange experience for him. He wasn't used to this armor yet and wasn't sure he ever would be used to it. But he'd been waiting for this opportunity. And now that it was finally here, he wasn't going to screw it up.

He was glad Kuroki was part of the team. Even though he'd never gotten much of a chance to know her when they were stationed together, she possessed a certain quality that made him want to trust her. Yoshida seemed like a decent sort—at least for a commanding officer. Though Masao had no clue why a guy from such a powerful family would be serving in the Tokkei instead of just living off his family's money.

And then there was Sayuri Tanaka. Lots of whispers and rumors about her. She had apparently gone to one of the most prestigious military academies and word was she had done some wetworks after graduating but before joining the Tokkei. The way she spoke was cold and direct, and it gave Masao an uncomfortable feeling being around her.

"We're ready," said Sayuri once she completed her call. "Yoshida and Kuroki are trying to find a way in, so while they do their job, we should do this fast."

Masao nodded. Sayuri darted across the roof and sprung just before she ran off the edge. Her figure soared across the gap, maintaining a graceful pose before she landed without a sound on the balcony. She glanced back at him and nodded, then he watched as she entered through the balcony.

"Right, time to do this…" Masao took a deep breath and ran. His eyes were fixed on the AR-HUD. The implants informed him that he was at the correct speed. And when the display told him to jump, he did.

His arms and legs flailed as he flew over the alley. The balcony was just ahead and he reached for it. The jump was just slightly short. He must not have done it at the right moment or jumped too soon. But his hand grabbed hold of the balcony railing. The nanites that made up the armor clung to the railing with an iron grip.

Masao pulled himself over the railing and stood on the balcony. He mentally scolded himself and was relieved that at least Sayuri had already entered, so she didn't see his performance.

Heavy blackout curtains prevented Masao from seeing anything inside the room. He activated the infrared sights and stared through the doors. In the adjacent room, he saw Sayuri's figure moving through quietly, approaching the doors. The infrared showed a few guards patrolling the halls and Sayuri left the room to start taking them out.

Masao looked inside the room his balcony was connected to and there was a figure lying on his back. That had to be Kitano. Masao placed his hand on the sliding door and the nanites scrambled the biometrics on the electronic lock. The door automatically slid to the side and Masao carefully stepped in the room.

The man lying in bed was older with graying hair. The AR-HUD's facial recognition kicked in automatically, matching him to the photo in the Tokkei's database. A list of crimes he had been arrested for or was suspected of involvement in scrolled over Masao's display.

"Here we go…" he muttered and slowly approached

the bedside. Masao's eyes went around the room once more, using his infrared to try and spot Sayuri. A number of the guards were now lying on the floor. Their body temperature had already started to fall, and it didn't take much for Masao to understand why.

Kitano snored loudly and shifted in bed. The nightstand housed a bottle of Jack Daniel's that was almost empty. Seemed Kitano was sleeping off a hangover, which made this operation even easier.

Masao reached for a container on his armor. Inside were three small needles, each one containing the right amount of sedative necessary to knock Kitano out until they returned to the Ministry. Masao examined one of the needles, then jammed it into the side of Kitano's neck. His eyes opened at the prick, but they quickly became heavy once Masao released the sedative.

"Package secure," said Masao, picking up Kitano and throwing him over his shoulder. "Do you—?"

There was the sound of a *thump* just outside the door. Masao readied his sword and activated the energy blade. That was when the door opened and Sayuri stood there. At her feet was a dead guard.

"Good, let's go," said Sayuri. "I'm in touch with homebase. There's a transport en route a few blocks away."

She went to the balcony door and jumped across the street without another thought. Masao watched her move and then crossed over himself. He didn't want to think about those guards Sayuri had killed. No doubt they deserved it—after all, they were yakuza. But he didn't have to feel that great about it. Though he was forced to ask himself what would she have done if she encountered someone who wasn't a guard, but one of the girls Kitano employs.

Masao put that out of his mind. He didn't want to think of what Sayuri was capable of, nor did he want to confront the issue of just what sort of operation he'd gotten himself mixed up with.

He only hoped the pay-off would be worth it in the long run.

CHAPTER 6

Erika ducked back into the server room as soon as her scanners alerted her they weren't alone. She saw Hiro was in the process of downloading the data from the hard drives. Part of her thought she should warn him. But then another part told her that she needed to do this on her own, prove herself worthy of this new position.

Besides, with this armor and her implants, what was there to worry about? Hiro said Kitano's men had received implants, too, but there wasn't any possible way they'd be as advanced as Tokkei tech.

She moved back into the corridor and kept her scanners running. Erika pressed her body up against the wall as she moved down, peeking into the different rooms as she passed.

First room, clear.

Second, clear.

Third, clear.

She kept moving from room to room, but her sensors

weren't picking up the motion again. Erika scolded herself for getting worked up over something that was probably nothing more than a rat. It was a good thing she didn't interrupt Hiro—he probably would have laughed at her for letting this place affect her so much.

But then her sensors alerted her to movement again. And now she was close enough that her audio enhancements were picking something up. She still wasn't close enough to make it out, but she could tell where it was coming from. Erika's AR-HUD indicated the direction and she came to a T-junction in the corridor. She peered around the corner and saw it was clear. Her hands tightened around the sword's hilt.

She'd been in countless battles before, back during her time in the Jietai. But this was different. A mixture of excitement to prove herself and uncertainty about relying on technology she'd only just been introduced to.

A room door was closed. But audio was leaking forth from there. Someone was in there. In fact, now that she was closer, her audio implants were picking up two distinct individuals. She could take out a pair of thugs without backup.

Erika moved in front of the closed door. She activated the tsuka, and the energy blade flared to life, forming into the perfect shape of a katana. Erika confirmed on her AR-HUD that it was set to the maximum setting, then charged at the door.

The energy blade sliced through the metal like it was nothing. She knew the mandate was stealth, but two she could take out quickly and without incident. Shouts of surprise and protest came from the two as they turned to face her. They were dressed in dark suits and had on sunglasses, and they were armed with guns.

Both opened fire. With the aid of her implants, Erika's reflexes became almost preternatural. Her sword easily cut through most of the bullets flying at her. A few got past, but they flattened against her impenetrable armor.

"Tokkei," said one of the two to his partner. "We have to get out of here!"

"What about him?" asked the other.

"Forget him, go!"

"You're not going anywhere!" shouted Erika.

They didn't respond and instead retreated back into the shadows behind them. Erika gave chase, but as she approached the shadows, another sound emerged. Rapid movement blared on her AR-HUD, but it wasn't enough of a warning and something slammed into Erika.

She was thrown clear across the room, hitting the far wall. Erika slumped on the ground and slowly raised her head. Behind her faceplate, her eyes went as wide as saucers. And she saw just what was being hidden down here.

It was human—or at least part of it was. There were certainly human-esque parts attached to it. But they were fused with metal. Skin had been stretched across machinery and it looked at her with a pair of eyes—one mechanical, one human. It stood over six feet tall and seemed like something out of a horror movie. Erika had to shut down her olfactory implants to prevent the stench of rotting flesh and motor oil from infecting her nostrils. Just what was Kitano *doing* down here? This was far beyond anything she could have expected.

The unholy amalgam of man and machine uttered what Erika could only describe as a scream, but the sound was unlike anything she'd ever heard before. Some sort of soulless marriage of tearing metal and a wailing animal, and when she heard it, every single hair on the back of her neck stood at attention.

"Keep it together, Kuroki," she whispered to herself, and that brief encouragement did provide some comfort. The sword was still set to kill, and she figured that would be the minimum necessary to take this…thing out. But she still had doubts even if that would work.

Erika ran at him, and the beast swung a massive arm towards her. The room wasn't very large, so it was nearly impossible to avoid him. Her back hit the wall, and he was on her. His hand, like a giant metal claw, pinned her to that spot, her sword now held uselessly at her side.

She deactivated the blade and tried to turn the tsuka. The beast kept screeching at her with that inhuman wail. If she could angle the blade just right, she might have a shot. But if she was off, then she'd learn real quick whether or not this armor could withstand its own weapons.

Erika had the tsuka in position and activated the weapon. The energy blade stabbed right into the creature's arm and he wailed. His grip loosened enough for Erika to squirm out of his reach. She wondered if she could make it to the door faster than the creature could move.

Making a break for the exit was a big risk, but Erika reasoned it was less of one than staying in here with that thing. As she expected, he did attempt to lunge for her again, but this time she was prepared. She ducked under his swing, sliding on the ground. Erika held the tsuka up and the blade sliced through the arm, severing it just between the wrist and elbow. It landed on the ground and Erika glanced back at it. There was a mixture of blood and oil seeping from the severed appendage.

The beast clearly wasn't happy about it, either, and he came after her. Erika ran through the door and back into the hall. She heard a crash and chanced a look over her shoulder to see that the beast was on her tail. The dimensions of the corridor were just barely enough to contain him and he moved after her in a hunched-over posture. Though for all Erika knew, that could be his natural posture.

"Kuroki, do you copy?"

It was Hiro's voice ringing through her communicator. She'd never been so happy to hear from someone before. "Yeah, I'm here."

"I'm just about finished here, but thought I heard some kind of noise. Did you pick up anything on your sweep?"

"You…*might* say that."

The beast roared again. Erika sprung, turning in mid-air and seeing the creature again. She landed and slid a few inches before coming to a stop. Erika activated the tsuka and readied herself.

"Do you need a hand or something?"

"I think I can handle it," she said. "Or…*hope* at least."

"What? Kuroki, now's not the time to—"

"I'll be with you in a minute."

Erika charged forward and leapt, blade first. It went right into the beast's chest and the two of them both fell back. She deactivated the blade and then turned it on again, this time plunging it into the creatures head.

"Sorry to cut you off, had to take care of something real quick," she said, her breathing a bit heavy from the fight.

Moments later, Hiro had arrived at her location. Erika leaned against the wall and motioned down at the beast. "That was what I found."

"Eh…what the hell…" Hiro stood in near shock for a

few seconds before finally kneeling down before the beast. "This was down here?"

"Yeah," she replied. "Found two guys watching it. They looked like they may have been Kitano's men."

"Did you stop them?"

"Unfortunately no, they got away while I was dealing with this guy."

"This is…unreal…" said Hiro. "I don't even know what to say about this."

"Can you get any readings off it?"

"Some, but not a whole lot right now. Think we'll have to take it with us back to HQ, try and get some answers from the lab guys." Hiro stood and turned away from the creature. He opened a comms channel. "Yoshida. We've got an unidentified cybernetic organism at the following coordinates. Bring a cleanup crew. It's not going to be pretty."

Once he ended the call, Erika spoke up. "Have you ever seen anything like this before?"

Hiro took a deep breath, but wouldn't look at the creature again. "No," he finally said after a long pause.

"Any idea just what Kitano was up to down here?"

"I've got a strong feeling this goes beyond Kitano," said Hiro. "There's something a lot worse happening down here, and I intend to find out just what's happening."

"Who would even *do* something like this to another human being?"

"If you knew all the horrors that were out there, you probably wouldn't sleep so well," said Hiro.

"And how do you sleep?" asked Erika.

He scoffed. "Never said I did." The joke failed to really ease the tension, so instead Hiro chose to change the subject. "What about the two guards? Did you get a good look at them?"

"Yeah, I think so."

"Perfect, we can run facial recognition on the footage from your helmet. With any luck, we'll be able to track them down. Very few places people can hide these days."

Hiro took one last, long look at the creature, then started walking away from it.

"Check in with the others, see if we're ready to get the hell out of here yet. Assuming everything went off without a hitch, they should get Kitano somewhere and wait for extraction."

There was something odd about his behavior, and Erika made a note of it. Hiro said he'd never seen something like this before. But that pause and how his body stiffened when he answered, it told Erika he knew something that he wasn't telling her. And then the crack about the horrors in the world. It didn't exactly put her at ease.

But she decided to file it away for later. They had more important things to focus on at the moment, and Erika wasn't about to screw that up just because of some doubts. Besides, those doubts were likely unfounded to begin with. She simply had an overactive imagination.

"Tanaka, Ishiyama, either of you copy?" she asked on the comms channel.

"Tanaka here," came Sayuri's voice. "We're all set on our end."

"The package?"

"One tattooed piece of shit all giftwrapped and ready for delivery," was Masao's gruff reply.

"Good, Yoshida wants us to head back to HQ. Once

you get the package to a secure location, standby and await extraction."

"Understood," said Tanaka. "How'd things go on your end?"

"That's…a long story," said Erika. "We'll discuss it back at base."

"Copy that. See you back at the ranch. Tanaka out."

Erika closed the comms channel herself and saw Hiro had already moved pretty far from her. His locator blipped on her AR-HUD and she quickened her pace to catch up with him at the entrance to the basement. The nanites retreated from his body and back into the container, revealing his street clothes.

"We good?" he asked. There was something about his eyes, a coldness she hadn't really seen before. Whatever that thing was, it clearly threw Hiro off his game to some extent.

Erika deactivated her own armor and nodded once the nanites were gone. "They'll get him secure and then wait for extraction."

"Good. You and I are going back on foot. Let's go."

CHAPTER 7

Hiro didn't say a word on the trip back to headquarters, and Erika didn't feel comfortable enough pressing him on the matter, so she kept her own concerns to herself. Once they got back, they could dig into the files Hiro had downloaded as well as figure out just what that thing was and how Kitano was involved.

Back at HQ, Sayuri and Masao were waiting for them. Their extraction had apparently come faster than it took for Hiro and Erika to return on train. Hiro didn't waste any time on formalities and walked up to the two-way glass that separated them from Junichi Kitano.

He had a day's growth of stubble on his face and his graying hair was toussled. He was dressed in blue silk pajamas, and the chair he sat in was anchored to the floor with restraints tying his wrists and ankles to the armrests and legs. He looked groggy and disoriented, but otherwise there weren't any visible bruises or injuries.

"How did it go?" asked Hiro.

"Pretty smooth," said Masao. "Sayuri took out…the guards quickly and quietly, then I nabbed Kitano right outta bed."

"Any problems?"

"Nah, I drugged him first. Just started to wear off, so he's still a little out of it. Could smell whiskey on his breath, too, which means chances are high he was hung over to begin with." Masao looked away from Kitano and down at Hiro. "How'd thing's go on your end?"

"Fine," said Hiro. "I've uploaded the data to HQ's server. Go down to analysis and let me know what they find."

"Can't they just let you know when they finish?" asked Masao.

Masao was taller, but the glare Hiro gave his subordinate seemed to make him shrink by at least a foot.

"Are you questioning me, Ishiyama?"

"N-no, nothing like that," said Masao. "I just thought I might be more use to you interrogating Kitano."

"No, I can handle him on my own. I want you to wait on the data analysis."

"Yeah, sure thing, you're the boss…"

Masao turned away and exchanged glances with both Erika and Sayuri that indicated his confusion. He left the three of them behind as Hiro resumed staring at Kitano through the glass. Erika and Sayuri also exchanged looks between each other to confirm they were just as confused as Masao. But Erika certainly didn't feel comfortable questioning their leader, and she could tell from Sayuri's own expression that the feeling was mutual.

"Kuroki and Tanaka, I want you to head to the lab," said Hiro. "They should be bringing in the remains soon, and I want to know just what the hell that thing was."

"You don't need any help here?" asked Erika.

There was a beat of silence that made Erika question the wisdom of even opening her mouth. And then Hiro spoke, which confirmed she was better off staying silent.

"Kuroki, I'm not some greenhorn. I was interrogating prisoners back when you were still learning the right way to hold a gun. I *know* what I'm doing."

"Yes, sir, of course. Tanaka and I will head to the lab." Erika bowed, even though Hiro hadn't turned away from the glass. Sayuri followed suit and then the two of them left the room together.

They walked down to the elevator and once they got inside, Erika asked the AI to take them to the research level. The doors closed and that was when Sayuri finally decided to speak.

"That was harsh," she said. "Both to you and Masao."

"We saw something in that basement," said Erika.

"What?"

"Seems Kitano was involved with some really twisted shit."

"What did you find?" asked Sayuri. "Corpses?"

Erika shook her head. "No. I mean…not exactly. It was…I don't even know if it was human anymore. You'll see for yourself when we get to the lab."

The elevator came to a stop and the doors parted. The two women walked down the corridor and continued on to one pair of large, metal doors. The scanner mounted above the doorway ran a check on both, and then the doors parted. A middle-aged woman in a lab coat with her hair tied back in a bun approached the pair, looking at them through small, wire-rimmed glasses.

"Agents Kuroki and Tanaka," she said, before offering a

bow. "My name is Dr. Iwata, I'm in charge of the biological research division here at the Ministry. I was told to expect you."

"Told?" asked Sayuri.

"Yes, Agent Yoshida just informed me you were on your way," said Iwata.

"Has the body arrived?" asked Erika.

"The team brought it in just a few minutes ago," said Iwata. "Unfortunately, I haven't yet had the opportunity to perform any examination."

"Show it to us anyway."

"Are you certain?"

"Positive."

"As you wish. This way, please."

Iwata turned and motioned for them to follow. They entered an adjoining room with refrigeration built into the wall and gurneys lined up in front of them. Only one of the gurneys was occupied, with the creature Erika had fought.

In the brief time Erika had known her, Sayuri Tanaka had always projected an air of absolute calm under pressure. Nothing seemed to rattle the woman. But that all changed the minute she laid eyes on the strange melding of man and machine, and her reaction was a gasp. It wasn't a massive reaction, but still more than Erika had come to expect of her teammate.

"What…what *is* that?" she asked.

"It's what we found—*I* found—in the basement," said Erika. "There were two guards watching over it, but they escaped."

"That still doesn't answer my question," said Sayuri.

"The mission briefing indicates that Kitano was in-volved in black market cyber-implants," said Iwata. "There's a high degree of risk involved in them. And many of the clinics have been trying to improve their methods. That leads to a lot of experimentation. And they don't exactly have a governing medical board to keep them in line, nor the knowledge of when they're going too far."

"You think this was one of those experiments gone wrong?" asked Erika.

"Quite possibly. The rumor is that the gangs have been attempting to improve their existing ranks through un-orthodox cybernetic enhancements. A way to compensate for the government crackdown that's thinned their ranks and slowed recruitment."

"You said rumored…?" asked Sayuri.

"That's right," said Iwata. "A lot of this stuff is kept quiet from the public, so there's just a lot of innuendo and suspicions. I personally haven't seen much evidence to support those rumors myself."

"Until now," said Erika.

"I haven't gotten many details about what happened. Were either of you there?" asked Iwata.

"Kuroki was," said Sayuri. "She said she found it."

"And in what state did you find it?" asked Iwata.

"Pissed off," said Erika.

Iwata blinked a few times, her lips slightly parted. "It-it was *conscious?*"

Erika nodded. "And not very happy."

"Are you saying you actually *fought* that thing?" asked Sayuri.

"He was one tough bastard," said Erika. "To be honest, I didn't think I was going to get out of there alive."

"Please, tell me everything," said Iwata, stepping closer to Erika. Her eyes were practically lighting up, and she could barely contain her excitement. It was a reaction that unnerved Erika.

"Well...he—it was strong. But it didn't seem to really know how to use that strength." Erika's brows tightened as she recounted her experience. "In fact, didn't seem like it had any sort of strategy at all. It behaved almost like a cornered animal."

"Interesting..." said Iwata.

"It also...it sounded like it was in pain," said Erika. "It kept making this kind of screeching sound. Like nothing I'd ever heard before. I'm starting to think it wasn't really trying to attack me, but more like it was just panicking."

"Well, perhaps a DNA scan will provide some clues," said Iwata.

She pulled a tray of instruments over, one of which was a device with a needle on the end. She inserted it into the monster's flesh and after a few moments, it beeped. Iwata looked at the display, then turned it to show it to the two agents. The display read "NO MATCH."

"What does that mean?" asked Sayuri.

"It means there's no genetic match in the government databases," said Iwata.

"But that's not possible," said Sayuri. "Everyone's genetic information is catalogued. Anyone who hasn't been catalogued—"

"Is a non-entity in the eyes of the government," said Erika. "An illegal immigrant."

"Seems likely this organization was trying to perfect its procedures by testing it on illegals," said Iwata. "It makes sense, actually."

A pit formed in Erika's stomach in reaction to Iwata's cool response. "Why do you say that?"

"If the government has no record of their genetic information, then there's no way of determining the identity. They can easily be disposed of once the tests are complete and authorities have no way of tracing it back to the perpetrators. And there's no one to miss the victims, so the police don't receive any pressure from next of kin."

"She's right," said Sayuri.

"They're still people," said Erika.

"Well…yes, of course. But…" Iwata didn't elaborate any further. Erika didn't need her to, either. She knew just what the doctor meant. That was the second time Iwata made Erika feel uncomfortable.

"Is there anything you can find out from an examination?" asked Erika.

Iwata sighed and looked over the creature. "In terms of establishing an identity? Not much. I can determine their genetic background, which might narrow down where they may have come from. But you probably won't find that leads to anything helpful."

"Perform the autopsy anyway," said Erika. "Your department and cybernetics should work together on this. We need to find out what Kitano was trying to do."

"Of course. I'm quite interested to see just what modifications have been made to this poor devil," said Iwata. "I'll contact you as soon as I've got the results."

"Thank you, Doctor." Erika bowed and left the morgue, with Sayuri following suit.

Erika just wanted to get out of there as soon as possible. She left the research lab and went into the corridor towards the elevator. Sayuri caught up with her while she was waiting for the elevator to arrive.

"Are you okay?" she asked.

"Yeah." Erika paused, then sighed. "No. I don't like that woman."

"Don't take it the wrong way. She's probably just…off. When you have a job like that, you probably see everyone as a potential science experiment instead of an actual human being. I've known people like that before. They don't mean to be off-putting, something about them just doesn't work the way it does in normal people."

"Maybe you're right. Still…something about her…"

"Look, let's just head back to Yoshida. Maybe he's gotten something out of Kitano by now. Something we can use."

"Yeah, let's do that," said Erika. "I've seen enough horror for one day."

The elevator doors opened and they both stepped inside. As it started moving, Sayuri asked the question that Erika assumed had been on her mind ever since she saw the creature.

"What was it like? Fighting that thing?"

"It was absolutely terrifying," said Erika.

"I wonder…"

"Wonder what?"

"Nothing, just curious what it would have been like. To be able to cut loose with your armor against something like that."

"Sayuri, if you had to go up against one of those things, you'd quickly wish you had never said that. It was not at all a fun experience. The entire time, I thought I was going to die. All I could think was…"

She stopped. Sayuri prodded her for more. "Was what?"

"Forget it. It's over and done now. And if I'm lucky, I'll never have to face something like that again."

CHAPTER 8

Hiro closed the door to the interrogation room and looked at the prisoner. He slowly circled the chair, but the older man didn't seem the least bit impressed by Hiro's movements. But Hiro didn't speak. He just kept on circling, barely even glancing at Junichi Kitano.

"So this is your plan, huh?" asked Kitano, finally breaking the ice. "You think making me dizzy is going to get me to tell you whatever it is you want to know?"

"I was hoping your sense of civic duty might get you to confess to your crimes," said Hiro. "And tell me what else I want to know about your little syndicate."

"Nothing to tell," said Kitano. "I'm a legitimate businessman."

Hiro couldn't restrain the laugh that escaped his mouth. "Really? You expect me to believe *that* crap?"

"You can believe whatever you want. Soon as I get a phone, I'll be making two calls. First one's to the governor so he can then tear your superiors a new asshole. Second one's to my lawyer so I can bring the mother of all wrongful arrest lawsuits against the government."

Hiro grinned. "You think the governor has any sway over me or my superiors? If I told the governor to go on national TV tomorrow and announce that the only way he can achieve an erection is by drowning kittens, he'd sprint to the nearest camera. Because the blackmail material my organization has on him would be far, far worse."

A slow realization crept upon Kitano's face. Hiro had to restrain himself from giving any kind of expression that would reveal just how much pleasure he took in that. This wasn't the first time Hiro had questioned some asshole who thought he was untouchable. It always started the same way—they throw their arrogance around and act like they couldn't care less about their situation.

And then, after Hiro set them straight, they always turned into blubbering cowards willing to sell out their own grandmothers for some leniency.

"Shit…you're lying…" said Kitano, though the horror on his face showed he knew Hiro was telling the truth. "There's no way you're Tokkei. You can't be…"

"Care to make a wager against that?"

"What do you want with me? Why would my business concern you?"

"As we speak, our analysts are going over the data we took from your drives. Once I receive a call, I'll know just what sort of shit you've been up to," said Hiro. "But what I want to ask you about now is that monstrosity I saw in your basement. A cybernetic experiment gone horribly wrong."

"I know what you're probably thinking, but you have to understand, I'm a patriot. What I did, I was doing for the good of the nation," said Kitano.

"And why should I believe that?"

"How do you think those fancy implants you boys wear are perfected? Through illegal black market experiments, the kind of which my organization provides the means for. I'm the troubleshooting department. We handle the trial and error aspect so you guys can keep your hands clean."

With a thought, Hiro cybernetically commanded the nanites to armor up his fist. He swung his arm and the nanites slid into place a fraction of a second before his fist connected with Kitano's jaw. The man's head snapped to the side with such force, anyone would be forgiven for being surprised that it didn't fly right off. Kitano turned his head and looked up at Hiro. He worked his jaw from side to side before spitting. Pieces of a broken tooth hit the ground at Hiro's feet, covered in blood.

"That fucking hurt!" shouted Kitano. "Listen kid, I'm cooperating here. Telling you the truth. At least as much truth as I can tell."

"Who was the test subject?" asked Hiro. "How did you even get the means to perform something like this?"

"The subject was a nobody, a non-person! Why the hell do you give a damn about them?"

"That thing I saw, it *was* a person. Once upon a time. Before you butchered him."

Kitano shook his head and chuckled. "You're unbelievable. Your bosses treat those people like sub-human and they spread propaganda that reinforces that belief, but now you want to hold *me* to a higher standard?"

"What are you talking about?"

"Refugees. Illegals. Sacrificed in the pursuit of advancing the nation."

Hiro struck Kitano again. "I don't know where the hell

you get off pretending like your barbarism is doing this country a favor."

"The pursuit of progress has always been on the backs of the dregs of society. You should study your history a little better."

Hiro was ready to deliver another blow, when he got a notice of an incoming communication. He left the interrogation room and went around to the adjoining monitor room. Erika, Sayuri, and Masao were all waiting for him.

"Are you doing okay?" asked Erika.

"I'm fine." Hiro's response was curt. "Tell me you've found something."

"It was human, at least at one point," said Sayuri. "But no genetic records on file. Further testing would have to be done, but seems obvious we're dealing with someone in the country illegally."

"I know, Kitano said the same thing," said Hiro. "What about the data? Have the analysts turned up anything useful?"

"Not quite yet, they're still working at it," said Masao.

"What the hell's taking them so damn long?" asked Hiro.

"It's encrypted."

"So? You're telling me the Tokkei doesn't have the means to break some yakuza syndicate's encryption?"

"If that's what we were dealing with, they'd have broken it already," said Masao. "Boss, what we're dealing with...it's military-grade encryption."

"That doesn't make sense," said Erika. "Kitano just runs an offshoot of the Yamazaki-gumi, and they wouldn't have the resources for something like that."

"Maybe that's the point. What we're dealing with is

a lot bigger than just some tattooed thugs." Hiro looked through the two-way divider at Kitano. "I'm going back in there to get some answers."

"You sure about that?" asked Erika. "Maybe one of us should give it a try."

"No, I've got it."

Hiro left his three subordinates and went back into the interrogation room. He closed the door behind him and then looked at the mirror on the wall, knowing the others were watching him from the other side.

"Enable privacy mode," said Hiro.

The room's system confirmed his voice and locked the door, while a screen slid over the mirror to block anyone from seeing what went on inside. Kitano looked around the room.

"No cameras in this room, Kitano. Soundproof walls. Mag-locked doors. And the only view from outside..." Hiro pointed to the covered mirror, "...has been obscured."

"So that's how it's going to be, huh?" asked Kitano.

Hiro nodded as the nanites flowed over his body, encasing him in his armor.

"I want to know everything about your little operation. Including how a bottom-feeder like you gets his hands on military-grade encryption."

"And you're going to torture me for the information?" Kitano shook his head. "Boy, you already *know* how I got that encryption. Just like you know who those experiments are done on behalf of. But you're not after truth today. You're after a cover story."

"That's what you think." Hiro took the tsuka in hand and activated it, a blade of crimson energy erupting from the device. "So we can do this the easy way, or we can do it the hard way. And just between you and me, after what I saw you did to that poor creature, I'm hoping you opt for the hard way."

浪人

Erika felt a great sense of unease when Hiro had left. She watched Kitano through the mirror, hoping Hiro would remember the mission and not lose control. But when he closed the divider, she knew things were serious.

"We have to get him out of there!"

She started to go for the door, but Sayuri grabbed her wrist. Erika turned and gave her teammate an incredulous look.

"What are you doing, Tanaka? Yoshida's obviously not in his right mind."

"Yoshida is our superior and he gave us an order," said Sayuri. "We have to trust in his wisdom to do what's right."

"He already roughed up Kitano. But after what we told him, he seemed determined to learn more, no matter the cost."

"Don't get in the way, Kuroki," said Sayuri. "Trust me on this."

Erika shook her head and wrenched her arm away from Sayuri's grasp. "Sorry, but I can't just let this happen." She was about to go for the door, but now Masao stood between her and it, arms folded over his chest.

"I'm sorry, Kuroki, but she's right. We have to let Yoshida handle this his own way."

"And what if his own way ends up killing the best lead we've got?" asked Erika. "You want to forget about the ethics, fine. Just think practically. How are we going to get to the bottom of this if Kitano's dead?"

The door opened from behind Masao. All eyes fell on Hiro as he entered the room. That cold, faraway look Erika had seen in Yoshiwara was back. Hiro didn't even make eye contact with any of them.

"Ishiyama, go back upstairs. Tell the analysts to put everything they've got on breaking that encryption. I want constant updates," said Hiro.

"Yessir," said Masao, then bowed and left.

"Tanaka, you're on Dr. Iwata. I want a full work-up on that poor devil and step on it."

"Understood, sir." Sayuri bowed and also took her leave.

"Kuroki, run facial recognition on the footage of everyone you encountered at Kitano's place. I want to know who they are and where they are immediately," said Hiro.

"Sir, if you'll forgive me for speaking frankly…"

"We don't have time for discussions, Kuroki. You have your orders, so follow them."

"Very well, as you wish." Erika bowed and also went for the exit. But before she stepped through the doorway, she turned and glanced back at Hiro. "Sir, if you'll permit me one question. What will we do with Kitano now?"

"We won't be doing anything with him, Agent Kuroki." Hiro's voice was completely robotic. "Junichi Kitano didn't make it."

CHAPTER 9

Hiro's actions had left Erika with a feeling of unease, but there was nothing that could be done about it. All she could do was focus on her assignment. She ran a facial recognition program on the footage she uploaded of the two men she saw in the basement. They'd both managed to get away in the chaos, but with Kitano dead, they were now the only leads she potentially had.

Fortunately, the database picked up a match for them fairly quickly. One of them was Tatsuo Watanabe and the other was Nobuo Takahashi. Both had criminal records for gang-related activities, but had somehow managed to get off with light prison sentences. Watanabe had no current address on record, but Takahashi did—an apartment in Shinjuku.

Erika went down there herself. She knew she should have readied backup—that was the proper protocol—but she was worried about Hiro's state of mind. And she wasn't very enthused by the way Sayuri and Masao just accepted his orders without question.

That was how she ended in the foyer of a tenement building in the heart of Shinjuku. The lobby entrance required a biometric check to enter, but she had ways around that. She activated the nanites to extend over her hand and placed it on the scanner. The display told her it was attempting to confirm her identity. Naturally she had no records on file, but the nanites could override most biometric security systems. After a few moments, the display changed to read "IDENTITY CONFIRMED."

The glass doors slid open and Erika entered the lobby. Rather than take the elevator, she opted for the stairs. Takahashi's apartment was only on the fourth floor so it wouldn't be much of a strain for her. She quickly jogged up the stairwell until she came to her destination. Erika activated her full armor to scan the corridor from behind the door. There was no one else in the hall.

She left the stairwell and moved to the unit number listed in Takahashi's file. When she came to it, she put her hand on the biometric scanner beside the door. Just as in the lobby, it took a moment before the nanites were able to override the security and then the door slid open.

Takahashi's apartment was very spartan. Just past the foyer was a small corridor off to the side that led to the bathroom and the toilet. The main corridor was short and led into the kitchen. She checked the refrigerator and found it well-stocked with cans of beer but not much else.

Past the kitchen was the living room. A flat-panel TV rested on a simple stand in the corner. The room also included a table in the middle of the room and a small couch. Judging by the empty Cup Noodles containers on the table, she assumed he wasn't much for home cooking.

A sliding door led to the bedroom. A simple twin bed, a chest of drawers, and a closet filled with suits on hangers. That was all she could find in his place. Though she did give it a search, she wasn't able to locate anything else that could help her.

She could hear something come from the front door of the apartment. Erika opened the balcony door and stepped outside, closing it behind her and moving out of sight. Her AR-HUD went into infrared mode and she watched as somebody entered the apartment, moving through it and into the bedroom. But there were no other signatures, which meant he was alone.

Erika followed him across the balcony as he left the bedroom and went into the living room. He sat on the couch and then came the sound of the TV. She heard the popping open of a can.

She stepped in front of the balcony window, still hidden by the curtains. Erika coiled her fist and smashed through the glass. Takahashi jumped, spilling the beer over his dress shirt.

"Shit!" he screamed.

He tried to scramble to get to his feet, but Erika was on him a second before he could do anything more. She grabbed him by the neck and slammed him against the wall, pinning him and holding him so his feet were just off the ground.

"Remember me?" she asked. "I'm the one you sicced your little science experiment on."

"I didn't do anything, I swear!"

She threw him across the room, right into the television set, the panel shattering from the impact and scattering shards all over the floor. Erika picked him up while he still writhed on the ground and held him above her at arm's length. The tsuka materialized in her free hand and the energy blade erupted. Though Erika's sensors registered an elevated heart rate, all she had to do was look at the way Takahashi's eyes were glued to the blade to know just how much he clearly feared it.

"This isn't going to end well for you," said Erika. "Your only option is to tell me everything you know. If you don't, then I might be forced to do something drastic."

"Shit…shitshitshit…" he kept muttering, his eyes still on the blade. "I didn't know about any of this, honest! This was just a job! I didn't want to do anything to them!"

"'Them'? You mean he wasn't the only one?"

Takahashi nodded furiously. "There were others. Test subjects."

"Who were they?"

"Refugees. They wanted to experiment on them. Boss just did what he was told."

"Told by whom? The Yamazaki-gumi?"

"Spooks, that's all I know. Once, I tried to ask questions. Boss told me I'd better keep my mouth shut if I knew what was good for me."

"Where did the refugees come from?"

"All over Asia. We smuggle them in on cargo ships. Pay off customs officers so they don't inspect the hold. Promise 'em jobs. Young men, they get sold to construction firms. Women to the *mizu-shôbai.*"

That term meant water trade—a euphemism to describe the nighttime entertainment industry. Which no doubt included *fûzoku* or the sex trade.

"Young men and women. But they're not the only

ones you smuggle in, are they? What about the elderly or children?"

"If they're too old or look like they're too old, or if they're weak or crippled, they become test subjects," said Takahashi. "As for the kids…you don't wanna know."

He didn't need to spell it out, Erika could read between the lines. And it only made her angrier. She threw him through the balcony door she'd shattered earlier and he struck the railing. It was the only thing that prevented him from falling to his death.

Erika held her sword right at his throat. All she wanted to do now was kill this scumbag. She was starting to understand the anger Hiro felt when dealing with Kitano. And she felt herself about to succumb to it as well.

"Stop!" Takahashi pleaded with her, pressing his body against the rail, trying to keep himself away from the sword. "That's not what we did with all of 'em."

"What are you talking about?"

"If you let me go, I can tell you where we took them," he said. "We took a few for our own experiments. But a lot were taken somewhere else. And you may not like what you find."

"You let me worry about that. Just tell me where you took them."

"One of the Izu islands. Hachijo-kojima. We load 'em up on a cargo ship and send them out there. No clue what happens once they leave the port."

"I found you once already," she said. "If you're lying about this, don't think I can't find you again. There's nowhere you can run in this country where I don't have eyes."

"I know, I know," said Takahashi. "I swear on my parents' grave, it's the truth."

"Where do the ships leave from?"

His lips moved, but for some reason, Erika couldn't hear his voice. She realized it wasn't just him—she couldn't hear anything happening outside her armor. She felt her arms lowering as the blade retracted, actions she had *not* intended to perform.

"What is this?" she asked, though she was certain her voice wasn't leaving the confines of her helmet. "What's going on?"

Takahashi gave her a perplexed stare as Erika's body backed away from him and jumped to the balcony above. Nanites flowed from Erika's fingertips, spreading out to adhere to the surface of the building. She wasn't even aware the armor had that capability.

Against her will, Erika scaled up the length of the tenement to the roof. Once she reached the surface, her helmet retreated from her face and she could move again. And she saw Hiro standing before her, also in armor with his helmet off. He held one arm perpendicular to his body and there was a holographic projection coming from his wrist—of Erika's armor. The projection vanished and he lowered his arm to look at her.

"*You* did that?" she asked.

"Your armor is Tokkei property, that means the Tokkei has the ability to commandeer and control it remotely."

Erika's natural response to that information was rage. She found her hands tightening into fists and it was all she could do to *not* launch an attack against her superior officer right then and there. Such a thing would no doubt mean an instant court-martial, so she kept herself reserved to just using words.

"You controlled me. Against my will. Do you have any

idea what that's like?"

Hiro avoided her hard stare. "Believe me, it's not something I enjoy doing. But you hardly gave me much of a choice."

"*Excuse* me? You told me to track down Kitano's men. I'm following your orders."

"Yes, track them down. Find out where they are and then bring that information to me," said Hiro. "I don't remember telling you to break into a guy's apartment and threaten him."

"How is that any different from what you did to Kitano?" she asked. "Or is this a case of 'do as I say and not as I do'?"

Hiro remained stoic, but she could see he was annoyed with her. The tightening of his lips, the knitting of his brows. Erika didn't care. His behavior with Kitano had annoyed her, and now this. Something just didn't smell right the situation.

"This job is over, Kuroki," he said.

"What?"

"You heard me. Please don't tell me I have to repeat myself."

"What makes you say the job's over?" she asked. "Like hell it is. Do you know what that asshole just told me? That guy we encountered was *not* the only one. They've been testing cybernetics on innocent people. He even said—"

"When I say a job is over, that means it's over," said Hiro, his voice growing firmer. "Orders from on high. Kitano is gone and without him, the rest of the network won't go far. We're through here."

Hiro raised his arm and a projection of a small aerial vehicle came from his wrist as well as controls. He manipulated the holographic controls until a light fell over them. Erika looked up and saw the exact same vehicle silently hovering above the building. It lowered closer to them and a hatch opened on its underside. Two cables lowered from the hatch and Hiro grabbed them both. He wrapped one around his arm and held the other out for her.

"Come on, we have to go back to base. Fortunately for you, I've covered for you, said I ordered you to follow a lead," he said. "In your report, you'll write that the lead was a dead end and then we'll put all this behind us."

"This isn't right and you know it."

Hiro stepped closer to her and lowered his voice to a whisper, albeit a harsh one. "Listen, Kuroki. If you know what's good for you and your career, you'll drop this right now. If the general found out you violated protocol and took a sophisticated suit of Tokkei armor worth billions of yen out without sanction, your ass would be rotting in a prison camp before you could even *think* of the words 'court-martial.' I'm doing you a favor here, so wise up and keep your damn mouth *shut*!"

Erika gave no response, just wrapped the cable around her arm as well. She couldn't even bring herself to look at Hiro right now. She'd trusted this man, believed him to be someone worthy of respect. Now she was seeing him as just a puppet who would do whatever he was told.

There was more going on here, and she knew she'd have to figure this out on her own.

CHAPTER 10

Erika was in a foul mood after what Hiro had done. He'd taken control of her armor without her permission, without even attempting to consult with her first. Commanding officer or not, he had no right to do that.

They didn't speak at all on the flight back to headquarters. Once they returned, Erika went to the Tokkei office on her own. The office had desks placed up against each other in rows. The workstations on the desks were flat plastic screens with cameras installed at the top. It was completely empty, save for Sayuri, who was busy at one of the workstations. Her fingers danced across the holographic keyboard, but she stopped and looked up when she heard Erika enter the room.

"Where did you run off to?"

"Yoshida had me checking a lead."

"Kitano's men?"

Erika nodded, remembering the story Hiro had told her to stick with. "Something like that. Didn't pan out, unfortunately. Just have to file the report and then I'm looking forward to heading home."

Sayuri blinked, staring at Erika while she sat at a workstation nearby. "You're going home?"

Erika felt puzzled by the question and she met Sayuri's confused stare. "Yeah, why?"

"Because tonight's our *kangeikai*. Remember?"

Erika sighed, her head sinking. She'd completely forgotten about the welcome party that was scheduled in honor of her, Sayuri, and Masao joining the team. Briefly, she wondered if she could find a way out of it by saying she wasn't feeling well, or that she wanted to finish up her training. She knew, however, there'd be no getting out of it. These parties were considered mandatory, particularly for new members.

"You don't seem that enthused," said Sayuri.

"I'm tired is all."

"Better suck it up. You especially can't afford to be seen as different."

"Excuse me?" asked Erika.

"It's nothing." Sayuri submitted her report and logged off from her workstation. The holographic keyboard vanished and her plastic screen went blank. She stood and went to the exit. "I'll see you tonight. The bus will pick us up from out front at nine. Don't forget that this constitutes an official military event."

She left the room and Erika shut her eyes briefly to compose her thoughts. *You especially can't afford to be seen as different.* Conformity was big in the government agencies, but particularly so in those that belonged to the Ministry of Defense. Sayuri's implication was clear—Erika's heritage.

Erika activated the terminal and the camera scanned

her face, confirming her identity via facial recognition and retinal scan. The holographic display appeared on the screen and the keyboard materialized to life in front of her.

She began work on the report, carefully noting everything Hiro had told her to say. She wrote that she'd been sent to investigate Nobuo Takahashi and that the lead had turned into a dead end. Takahashi was just a low-level enforcer with no useful intelligence to provide on Kitano's larger criminal empire.

Once she finished, she hit the submit button and then logged off. Erika looked up at the clock and saw it was already half past eight. She needed to hurry and change so she didn't end up late for the bus. Sayuri made a point to remind her that this was a formal military event, which meant they were expected to wear their dress uniforms. Fortunately, Erika had hers in her locker here at headquarters, so at least she was thankful she wouldn't have to try to find a way to run home, change, and get back in thirty minutes.

浪人

At the restaurant, there were three long tables in the tatami room, and the guests took their spot on either side. The seating consisted of small, square cushions laid out at each spot around the table. Bowls filled with broth sat on portable electric stoves and next to each bowl was a large plate with a small selection of meet and a larger selection of assorted vegetables. Each place setting had a bowl for the stew and a small, rectangular plate with a few pieces of sushi.

Everyone was expected to sit with their department. Field operatives were considered their own department and even amongst them, they were divided into smaller teams. She found herself beside Masao and across from Hiro. Sayuri was to Hiro's right, directly across from Masao. Hiro and Erika sat at the end of the table, but at the front of the room was a shorter table perpendicular to the rest. General Hojo sat there, with other department heads. It was the first time Erika had seen him in person.

Idle chatter began as people still found their places. Once everyone was seated, Hojo rose, as did the rest of the department heads. The small talk ended and everyone else stood as well.

"Would all *shinnyû-shain* please come to the front of the room and line up?"

The word meant new employees, so everyone who had just been hired or transferred into this branch did as they were told, lining up in front of their new coworkers. One by one, they were all expected to give a short self-introduction. Erika just remained still with a smile on her face, barely paying attention to most. The exceptions were her two teammates.

Masao was the first of them to give his introduction. He took a step forward and bowed before speaking. "I am Masao Ichiyama from Yamaguchi. Formerly of the Jietai, recently promoted to the Ministry. *Yoroshiku onegaiitashimasu.*" He concluded with a final bow, and then stepped back into line.

Simple and to the point. Masao wasn't one to waste time or mince words, and Erika could sympathize with his desire to just get this over with so they could eat.

Sayuri stepped forward and bowed, a smile on her face. "My name is Sayuri Tanaka. I come from Hiroshima and graduated from the National Defense Academy. I look forward to learning from the wealth of experience present in this room. *Yoroshiku onegaiitashimasu.*" She bowed again.

Erika noted that Sayuri hadn't mentioned anything about what she did between graduating from the NDA and joining the Tokkei. There was likely a reason for that.

Finally, it was her turn. Erika stepped forward and bowed. "I'm Erika Kuroki, from Shizuoka. I'm afraid I must be a let-down after following Ms. Tanaka and her background from such an esteemed and storied institution. I've just transferred from the Jietai and I look forward to providing my services. *Yoroshiku onegaiitashimasu.*" She bowed again and then stepped back.

The rest of the new arrivals continued their introductions, but Erika noticed that some eyes still lingered on her. She recognized that look—it was one she had grown up trying to ignore. They were wondering just how someone like her managed to get a position within the Ministry of Defense, in particular the Tokkei.

Once the introductions were completed, everyone returned to their places and Hojo took the floor once more. The restaurant's waitstaff brought out bottles of beer, sake, and shochu and set them out on the table. Drinks were poured first for the superiors by their subordinates. Erika took a bottle of beer and was about to offer to pour for Hiro, but before she could ask, Sayuri had already managed to.

"Hey, Kuroki?"

Erika looked at Masao, who gestured towards her glass with the beer. She smiled at him and held her glass out. He filled it and then she returned the favor. Nobody began drinking just yet, though. Hojo took his glass of sake and raised it into the air. Everyone rose and held up their own glasses.

"In the past few decades, our country has gone through many changes. We've had to once more endure the trials of war. But we emerged successful and have seen a new generation of warriors. You embody the *bushido* code passed down from the revered samurai of old, and I know under your honorable service, Japan will continue to prosper." Hojo held up his glass. "*Tenno heika banzai!*"

His cry of "long live the Emperor" was echoed by the rest of the room. Then he offered one final word—"*Kampai!*"—which concluded his toast. It was repeated and then everyone clinked their glasses against their neighbors' before drinking. With the toast completed, a round of applause followed and then everyone returned to their seats.

The rest of the night went by in a blur of tedium. Erika didn't make much of an effort to move from her spot and mingle with the people from other departments. The way they looked at her when she stood before them told her everything she needed to know about them. She'd spent years in the Jietai trying to win over the approval of superior and subordinate alike. Now that she had finally managed to make it to the Tokkei on her own merits, with the deck stacked against her, she chose to simply keep to herself.

Hiro seemed to have much of the same attitude, though obviously for different reasons. As heir to the biggest defense contractor in Japan, Erika suspected he must have been used to—and grown tired of—various department heads trying to curry favor with him.

He noticed she was looking at him and met her eyes. Erika immediately looked down and picked up her bowl, quickly using her chopsticks to scoop a few thin slices of pork into her mouth.

"Kuroki?"

He called her name, but she was still embarrassed to look up. After the second time he did so, she finally glanced at him again with apprehension. Hiro was holding the beer bottle up and gesturing towards her. Erika looked at her glass and saw it was almost empty.

"No, it's okay. I can—"

"Relax, Erika," he said. "It's a party."

Erika blushed and held up her glass, which he quickly refilled. She bowed her head and sipped her beer, then offered to return the favor. But Hiro held up his hand in polite refusal, then glanced towards the head table.

"If my math is correct, the General's on his fifth sake," said Hiro.

Erika looked and saw that the old man's face was almost the color of a ripe tomato. She suppressed a chuckle from sneaking past her lips.

"Assuming past is prologue, that means he'll be coming by in a few minutes and try to force me to drink with him," said Hiro.

"I guess it happens a lot?" she asked, finally finding some courage to speak.

Hiro nodded. "Once our time is up here, he'll insist we go to an after-party at some high-priced hostess bar. Then he'll subject my ears to his tortured renditions of Arashi and Bruce Springsteen."

That time, Erika chuckled. Hiro finished the last of his drink and then smiled.

"And tomorrow, I'll go into work and he won't remember one single second of tonight."

"Maybe that's a good thing," said Erika. "If he knew you'd seen him like that, he might have you killed."

They both grew quiet at that and looked down at their

bowls. Erika regretted having brought up something so grim, even though it was intended to be a joke. But in their line of work, such things wouldn't be surprising. Not even unheard of, for that matter.

Erika finished her bowl and refilled it with broth and just a few vegetables. As she did that, Hojo came around—just as Hiro had predicted. The general nearly fell down as he sat at the end of the table and set an unopened bottle of sake on the surface. His words were slurred as he poured a drink for Hiro.

"You…" said Hojo as he looked at Erika. He seemed to struggle to hold his eyelids up and his entire body moved like a blade of grass in the wind. "Wha's your name again…?"

"Kuroki, sir," said Erika and bowed her head.

"Ah, right. Kuroki." Hojo held up the bottle and brought it towards Erika's now-empty glass. "Here. Drink."

"Thank you, sir, but—"

"You…refusin' my hospitality?" He squinted as he stared at her. "Why's that…?"

"She's had a lot to drink already tonight, sir," said Hiro. "No one in the whole of the Tokkei has the stamina of the great General Hojo."

"Rightchoo are, Yoshida!" said Hojo with a laugh. He threw his head back so far, he almost lost his balance, but Hiro kept him sitting upright. Hojo leaned over the table, moving closer to Erika. His breath stank of sake and miso. "Maybe yer genes just ain't strong enough, eh Kuroki?"

There it was again. The reminder that no matter what she did, how much she fought to prove herself, they would still view her as less than any other agent. Just by virtue of who her father was.

"I guess you're right, sir." Erika set the bowl back on the table. Suddenly she'd lost her appetite. "If you'll excuse me, I have to use the restroom."

Erika stood and left the dining room. She walked down the hall to the restroom. There was a sink just outside the two toilet rooms and she turned on the faucet to splash some water on her face. Erika took a paper towel from the basket and patted her skin dry, staring at her face in the mirror. After a few deep breaths, she started the walk back down the hallway.

When she reached the dining room, she hesitated just as she was about to open the sliding door. Instead of returning, she decided that she wasn't yet ready to go back inside. So she continued walking down the hallway, to the narrow staircase and descended it to the first floor.

There was a counter bar and high-backed booths. The restaurant was filled to capacity, and drunken laughter and conversation bounced all over the room. The scent of grilled fish and meat lingered in the air, accompanied by a haze of grease-stained smoke. Erika finally found the exit and stepped outside.

Even though they were in the Ginza neighborhood of Tokyo and there was plenty of activity going on all around, it still somehow felt a bit more peaceful out here.

"Kuroki?"

She looked up at the sound of her voice and saw Masao standing just a few feet away. Erika hadn't even realized he'd stepped outside until just then.

"What are you doing out here?" she asked.

Masao held up a vaporizer. "Just felt like a puff. How about you?"

"Needed some air." She moved closer to him and leaned

against the building's exterior.

"So…Tanaka said you went on some sort of job for Yoshida before the party?"

"Yeah, but it didn't lead to anything," she said. "Besides, I'm not interested in talking about our jobs right now."

"Okay, so what *do* you want to talk about?" he asked.

She shook her head. "I don't know. I just know this party is boring me to tears and I want to get away."

"I think I've got a solution to that," said Masao.

Erika looked at him with confusion. "What's that?"

CHAPTER 11

The feel of sunlight on her face stirred Erika awake. She stared at the window, the sun beginning to rise over the view of the Tokyo skyline. It took a few moments, but eventually she realized that this view was *not* the one from her apartment.

Erika sat up in bed with a start, and that sudden movement caused her head to scream at her in pain. She wrapped her arms around herself, feeling a chill, and then she noticed she was naked. Her smartwatch read that it was just before six.

There was a sound coming from the side and that's when she noticed the figure under the sheets next to her, sleeping on his chest. His head was turned away and Erika was afraid to turn his face to see who he was. She slid carefully out from under the sheets.

The components of her dress uniform were scattered across the room. She dressed quickly, stopping after pulling on the slacks and buttoning the shirt. No need to don the jacket or cap.

Part of her considered just walking out, but she wanted to know. Erika circled around to the other side of the bed so she could view the man's face. She groaned when she saw it was Masao.

She strained her memory. Flashes of the night before started coming to her. After her and Masao spoke outside the restaurant, they went back inside and he acted as if he was dead drunk, stumbling all over the private dining room. Erika had played her part of the concerned coworker and Hiro told them to go ahead and leave.

But then what happened? The memories continued to trickle in, and she remembered how they began walking towards the train station. They passed by a late-night ramen shop and stopped in. While eating, they got the itch to head to a karaoke spot.

That was when the night started to blur. They chose the *nomihodai* or open bar plan. Three hours of singing and knocking back beers and highballs alone in a room together gave them a chance to really get to know one another. At one point, she remembered initiating the first kiss. This was apparently what it led to.

"Kuroki…?"

Erika was startled by the sound of her name. She looked at Masao, who struggled to open his eyes and opened and closed his mouth, appearing like his mouth felt akin to a desert. Masao sat up and rubbed his eyes, then looked at her. It took him a few moments to process what was happening.

"How much did we drink…?" he asked.

"*Too* much by the looks of it." She groaned.

He yawned deeply and then said, "I'll try not to take that personally."

She sighed. "That's not what I meant. This is just…I don't think it's a good idea to get involved with someone I work with."

"It's fine." He climbed out of bed and Erika turned her back on him. He chuckled and added, "*Now* you're acting shy?"

"Look, I'm…going to go…"

"Hold up." He grabbed her arm just as she started to move for the door. "Look, you're here anyway, why don't you stick around for a bit and have some breakfast?"

"Thanks, but I should really go," said Erika. "I have to get home, shower, and get a fresh change of clothes before going to HQ."

"You gonna have enough time?"

She nodded. "I'll call a taxi." Erika moved for the door, but stopped before walking out. "Ishiyama…when I say I don't want to get involved with anyone at work…"

"You also mean you don't want anyone to know about this," said Masao.

Erika turned around and was relieved to see that Masao had pulled on a *yukata*. "Yes. Again, it's nothing personal—"

"I get it," he said. "This is just something that happened. There's no need for us to dwell on it. And don't worry, I'm not some office gossip. Nobody will hear anything from me."

She smiled. "Thank you. I appreciate it."

Erika went from the bedroom into the small adjoining kitchen. There were some empty beer cans on the counter, and she wasn't quite sure if those were Masao's from earlier or if they'd had some extra drinks after leaving karaoke.

She found her shoes in the foyer and quickly pulled

them on, carrying her uniform jacket and hat bundled under her arm. Like most apartment buildings, the corridor was open-air. Erika went to the elevator, seeing she was on the eighth floor and pushed the call button.

While she rode the elevator down to the ground floor, she tapped her smartwatch twice to activate the heads-up display on her augmented reality implant. Erika used her hands to manipulate the menu projected on her retina, sending a message for a taxi service. Once she finished, she closed the AR-HUD by tapping her smartwatch again.

Erika got off the elevator and left the building to wait by the curb. Fortunately a taxi must have been nearby because it only took a few moments for one to arrive. The taxi—like all vehicles—hovered just slightly off the ground, and the door rose up. Erika climbed into the car. There was a display on the window that showed the map, with both her current position and the destination she'd programmed when summoning the cab. All taxis in Tokyo at least were self-driving, so there was no driver. There were manual driving controls, but they were all locked down by the cab company.

The car began its journey. Erika sighed and rested her head against the seat. She wanted to just climb into bed and pass out for several hours. But calling in sick after leaving the party early with Masao would raise a lot of rumors. She had to suck it up and make it through the day.

Masao's place fortunately wasn't too far from her own. In fact, they both lived in the Minato ward. That was some cause for relief. Meant the drive took just about fifteen minutes. She'd be able to shower, dress, and have at least something to eat before ordering a new cab to get to work.

The cab pulled up to the curb just outside her apartment and the door opened for Erika. She went to the lobby entrance and touched her thumb to the scanner, then looked into a flashing red light for a retinal scan. The doors slid open and she took the elevator to her apartment on the fifteenth floor. Biometrics again were used for the locks on her unit and she finally returned home.

Her apartment was almost entirely white, almost like a surgical suite. All government employees were provided with free housing. Hers was a standard 1LDK—a one-bedroom unit with a kitchen and a living and dining room. What little furnishings the apartment had were provided when she moved in—she never bothered to buy anything extra. While in the Jietai, she could be stationed anywhere in the country—or even the world, so she became accustomed to living a spartan existence.

Erika went to the bathroom and dropped the clothes under her arm on the floor. She quickly took the rest of her clothes off and got into the shower to quickly clean off.

As she felt the hot water strike her body, her mind kept drifting to the previous night. Masao was a good guy, but Erika felt nothing for him beyond friendly affection. Getting involved with him would prove a mistake if she continued down that path. He seemed to understand and she hoped that would be the end of it.

But there was a nagging thought at the back of her head. One that kept asking a multitude of questions, each beginning with the words "what if." What if Masao did let it slip to someone else at work? What if he didn't simply take no for an answer and try to pursue her? What if Hiro found out?

That last question gave her pause. Why would it matter more what Hiro thought than anyone else in particular?

She sighed and finished the shower, then quickly dressed in the standard Ministry uniform. The Tokkei was highly secretive, so when not in armor, they simply went to work in the same uniforms worn by other Ministry employees.

Barely a few weeks into her position and already she was running into problems with others on her team. Seemed she'd had some uncomfortable encounter with pretty much every single person in her immediate circle. Hiro, Sayuri, Hojo, and now even Masao. All in all, it seemed like a particularly poor way to make a good impression. She could only imagine how some of them—the general in particular—would treat it as a shortcoming due to her heritage.

Erika tied her hair back in a tight bun and stared into her own eyes in the mirror for a few moments. She had to put those thoughts out of her mind and just focus on proving herself.

"You've come too far to let doubt stop you," she said to her reflection. "Just persevere and keep striving for what you want."

CHAPTER 12

Erika arrived at HQ right on time and without any issues. She took her place at her workstation beside Sayuri and activated her terminal. Erika glanced at the desk across from her. That was where Masao sat, but he hadn't come in yet. As Erika went through the morning routine of checking for new messages, she could feel Sayuri's eyes on her. But whenever Erika chanced a look back, Sayuri remained focused on her terminal.

"Kuroki?"

"*Hai*!" Erika nearly jumped to attention from her desk and turned to the voice that had called her name. It was Hiro, standing near the office entrance and holding a cup of coffee in his hand.

"Would you mind following me? I'd like to speak with you."

Erika started to feel a pit in her stomach and she was worried this might have something to do with last night—either the party or the incident with Takahashi.

But she couldn't very well refuse a direct order from her commander, so she just nodded and followed him from the office. Hiro brought her to one of the briefing rooms and gestured for her to sit.

"There's something I'd like you to investigate," he said.

"Of course," said Erika. "What is it?"

"Have you ever heard of Kenjiro Miyata?"

Erika's eyes rolled up as she searched her memory for some recollection. When she came up with nothing, she shook her head. "No, I don't think so."

"He is—or was—a pioneer in cybernetic implants," said Hiro. "The Tokkei armor was one of his achievements."

"Okay…"

"But there's a problem," said Hiro. "You see, some new information has come to light from the…incident at Yoshiwara. Cybernetics examined the body and they believe that this technology carries Miyata's signature."

"You think he might have been involved with Kitano's operation," said Erika.

Hiro nodded. "We do. But there's a problem. Miyata went missing about two weeks ago. Timing seems pretty suspicious, wouldn't you agree?"

Erika gave a nod.

"I want you to find him and bring him in. If he's selling his technology on the black market, that could pose a massive threat to national security."

"Of course. But I don't understand. You want me to go after him on my own?" asked Erika.

"He's an old man, Kuroki, I don't think you'll have much trouble with him."

"That's not what I mean," said Erika. "Isn't it standard for new agents to be accompanied by a senior?"

Hiro sipped his coffee and then said, "Normally, yes. But under these circumstances, General Hojo feels a one-man operation would be better."

"Sir, can I ask why you aren't taking the job?"

Hiro looked down, and Erika could have sworn she saw his cheeks reddening just a bit. He sighed and then offered his explanation. "Conflict of interest."

"What? How?" she asked.

"Do you know where the Tokkei and the Jietai purchase most of their cybernetics?"

Erika took a breath and nodded. She understood now and she continued to look at Hiro even as he stared into his coffee. "Yoshida Technologies."

"Exactly. The company owned and operated by my family," said Hiro. "Miyata knows me personally. If he saw me, he'd know we were after him. Instead, I need someone I can trust to track him down."

Erika almost dreaded to ask her next question, but her curiosity got the better of her. "And is that someone me?"

Hiro met her gaze. "I'm asking you, aren't I?"

"Even after Takahashi?"

He sighed. "That was a stupid move. But I understand why you did it. I don't want any of that crap this time, though, okay? You find Miyata—however possible—and you bring him in for questioning."

"But why me? Why not Tanaka? She's certainly capable of this kind of job."

"Do you know what made you stand out enough to be promoted here?" asked Hiro.

Erika had no idea why he brought that up. "To be honest, I'd never given it much thought."

"Yes, you have," said Hiro. "Sayuri Tanaka is a great

fighter, very adept with weapons, and she has a strategic mind. But you know what she lacks?"

Erika shook her head.

"Imagination," said Hiro. "You tend to act more on instinct. Tanaka ignores her instincts and simply acts the way her instructors at the NDA told her to act. And I need someone with good instincts on this."

Th-thank you, sir," she said. "Of course, I'll do whatever's necessary to bring Miyata to justice."

Hiro nodded. "I know you will. But another thing, I don't want to advertise this to the rest of the department. This is a sensitive matter, especially as it involves my family's company. Statistically, the less people who know about something, the less chance it leaks. And if word that the top military contractor had a rogue engineer selling advanced techology on the black market got out to the press…"

He didn't have to finish, Erika knew what would happen next. It would mean a scandal of massive proportions for the government. Though the opposition parties in the Diet had mostly been weakened after decades of work by the ruling party, a scandal on this scale would probably galvanize their forces, maybe even get them to start joining together.

"I understand, sir. I'll be the model of discretion, you have my word."

"Good, the general will be glad to hear it," said Hiro. "Oh, and one more thing. About last night…"

Hiro stood and approached her. He stared into her eyes and then asked, "Was Ishiyama too much trouble to deal with? I hope he didn't put you out."

She sighed in relief. He didn't know. But still, she had difficulty looking at him when he brought up Masao.

"It was…fine."

"What happened?"

"Nothing. We both live in Minato, so we took the last train together, I helped him up to his apartment, and then I went home."

"I see."

"Is he…I didn't see him in the office…"

"He sent a message, said he'd be in later," said Hiro. "Sometimes, some of the new recruits can't hold their liquor, so it's not a surprise."

"Okay, well I'll get to work on finding Miyata."

Head to the cyberterrorism branch. I've already informed Shota Adachi to expect you. Speak to him and him alone. Remember, discretion is key."

She nodded. "Yes, I understand."

"Good."

CHAPTER 13

In order to begin the search for Miyata, the first thing Erika would have to do was run a tracer. Due to the close relationship between Yoshida Tech and the military, all the employees had to have their information registered with the government for national security purposes. According to privacy laws, the government was forbidden from using that information without a warrant.

But the language of the law and how matters were actually conducted in practice were two very different things. After all, racial and gender discrimination were technically also violations of Japanese law, but good luck finding a judge sympathetic enough to side with anyone who brought forward accusations of that nature.

The Ministry of Defense cyberterrorism division was located within HQ, and that was where Erika headed to immediately after leaving the meeting with Hiro. She was grateful to have an assignment that would get her out of the office, away from any questions that may linger after her and Masao left the party together. Hopefully by the time this case wrapped up, the whole thing would be forgotten.

The doors opened and Erika stepped off the elevator. There was a glass door with CYBERTERRORISM printed on its surface. A fingerprint scanner was by the side of the door. Erika placed her thumb on it and stared into the flashing retinal scanner.

"State your name and business," came an automated voice.

"Erika Kuroki, Tokkei Agent. I'm here to speak with Shota Adachi."

"One moment please."

The door slid open and the automated voice said, "Access granted. Please wait inside."

Erika stepped into the room. Cushioned benches lined the walls and there was one white door with no handle and no visible controls in the corner. She was alone, so she sat on the bench and waited. Erika blinked and brought up her AR-HUD. She had just begun reading through the news headlines, when the automated voice echoed in the room.

"Please refrain from using any network-connected implants while in our division. Thank you for your cooperation."

Erika sighed and closed the AR-HUD. Evidently, they took every precaution in this division when it came to visitors, even ones who had the clearance to be inside. Still, she did as she was told and waited quietly, crossing her legs and tapping rhythmically on her knee.

After a few minutes had passed, the door opened and Erika stood. The man in the doorway was middle-aged and wearing a white, short-sleeve dress shirt, black tie, and black slacks. His thinning hair had begun to gray at the temples and he wore glasses with black, plastic frames. A badge was pinned to his shirt pocket and it displayed his photograph and name. Had Erika spotted him on the street, she would have easily mistaken him for any run-of-the-mill salaryman as opposed to a cyberterrorism expert.

"Agent Kuroki, my name is Adachi," he said and then bowed. "Agent Yoshida told me to expect you. Please, follow me."

He turned and stepped back through the door. Erika followed him and they entered a hallway. There were doors off to the sides, but each one was closed off and they saw no one else as he led her through the maze of short corridors. There were no names on the doors, either. Adachi stopped at one of the doors and it opened for him immediately without any sort of prompt.

"Our implants are connected to our offices," said Adachi, answering her unspoken question. He gestured for Erika to enter first and she did. Once Adachi followed, the door closed behind him.

The back wall appeared to be a giant window, but when Erika examined the view, she tilted her head. It was historic Kyoto, she recognized it from a school trip when she was in junior high. But they were in the basement of the Defense HQ in Tokyo.

"I enjoy working with a view of Kyoto," said Adachi. "Due to the sensitive nature of our division, you can understand why any actual windows would be a bad idea. It's simply a video screen."

Adachi's desk had three sides and faced the screen. He took the seat behind and the holographic keyboard appeared on the surface. Once entering a command, panels on the floor shifted and rose, forming into a chair for Erika in front of the desk.

"Sit, please," he said as he went to work typing on the keyboard. Information was presented on the plastic monitor screens that lined each portion of his desk.

Erika sat at the desk and waited as he flipped and scrolled through information on the screens almost impossibly fast. She assumed he had implants designed to speed up his consumption of data. That was the only explanation for how he sifted through it so quickly.

"I trust Agent Yoshida told you why I'm here?" she finally asked after waiting several minutes in silence for him to say something.

"Yes, he did." Adachi gave no further information, just picked up the cup of coffee on his desk and sipped it while flipping through more information.

"So…do you have anything for me?"

He set the coffee back on the desk and with a wave of his hand, all the holographic data vanished from the plastic screens. Adachi now stared at her through those screens and offered a sigh.

"I am trying to do just that, Agent Kuroki. Unfortunately, it seems Dr. Miyata is rather difficult to find."

"But I thought all Yoshida employees have their information registered with the Ministry of Defense? Can't you simply track him through the neural network?"

"Normally yes, I would be able to do just that. And that is precisely what I've been trying to do so ever since Agent Yoshida contacted me first thing this morning," said Adachi. "Unfortunately, it doesn't seem to be that simple. Miyata seems to have gone off the grid."

As information technology started to explode in the early years of the twenty-first century, it became increasingly difficult, but not impossible for people to break away. But as that technology became increasingly one with the human body, now it seemed impossible.

"How?" she asked.

"The average person certainly couldn't do it. For someone as brilliant as Miyata, it would be incredibly difficult—and he would need money and help—but not impossible."

"How would he do it?" asked Erika.

"He'd need to remove any implants with a network connection and have them replaced with ones that have been scrubbed. And those aren't the kind of things that are easy to come by."

"He'd have to go to the black market for them, wouldn't he?" asked Erika.

Adachi nodded. "But that's just the start. Even after replacing the implants, there's still the matter of his genetic information. He would have to have it overwritten in order to truly begin a new life. Otherwise, he would run the risk of discovery."

"I've heard stories about overwriting, but I've never heard of an actual case. It is even possible?" asked Erika.

"The official position of the Japanese government is that genetic overwriting is a matter of pure science fiction."

"What about unofficially?"

Adachi grew silent and his lips tightened. He steepled his fingers as if deep in thought and leaned back in his black leather chair. After a few moments of consideration, he answered Erika's question.

"Yes, it's possible. Though incredibly risky and incredibly expensive. There is a high mortality rate attached to the procedure," he said. "If Miyata truly intended to disappear, he would need to take that step in order to guarantee no possibility of discovery."

"How long would all this take?" asked Erika. "Replacing the network implants, genetic overwriting, the whole process."

"The recovery time for such invasive procedures—should he survive—could take upwards of two months," said Adachi. "The priority would be the implants. He'd have to wait until after his body and mind recovered before he could attempt overwriting."

Hiro said Miyata had only been missing for two weeks. That meant there was still an opportunity for her to find him. She would need to dig deeper into his background, find out who might know something about him. He might even have been selling his tech on the black market in order to fund these procedures in the first place.

"Miyata was an important figure in Yoshida Tech, which meant he'd be a person of interest to the Defense Ministry. I need you to give me every bit of information the Ministry has on him. I have to dig into his life if I'm going to get some sense of where he might have gone to."

"Of course. Agent Yoshida already informed me that you would need such information, so I took the liberty of preparing it for you." Adachi went into one of his desk drawers and drew forth a small diskette, which he offered to Erika. "Everything we know about Kenjiro Miyata is written on that diskette. Download it right here to secure memory."

Erika took it in her hand. Her implants read the information on the diskette and downloaded it into her memory banks. She told her implants to perform encryption on it and they did as they were told, ensuring the data could not be siphoned by any pirates on the network.

Once the procedure was complete, she passed the diskette back to Adachi. He took it from her and crushed it in his hand into dust, then brushed the remains into a wastebasket under his desk.

"Thank you for coming down here, Agent Kuroki. Should I learn anything more, you will of course be the first person I contact. But for now, you may take your leave."

The door to Adachi's office opened, inviting Erika out to the hallway. She stood from the chair and it immediately collapsed, returning to the floor. Adachi was focused on his screens again and Erika had no other choice but to leave his office, following the corridor back to the waiting room in front.

She now knew every bit of information that the Defense Ministry possessed on Miyata. But if Adachi was right and he had gone through those procedures, Erika feared it might not be enough to locate him.

CHAPTER 14

The first thing on Erika's list was to investigate Miyata's home. He had a condo in Aoyama, one of the more upscale neighborhoods in Tokyo. For the investigation, Hiro had cleared her for use of a hovercycle, which would make it easier for her to get around quickly. She was glad for the time it spared more than anything else—public transportation would take her at least thirty minutes, but the hovercycle cut that time almost in half.

Her AR-HUD projected directions over her physical reality, signaling with large arrows when and where she had to turn. The cycle had AI control, but she seldom got the opportunity to drive one of these on her own, so she took advantage of the chance. Even though the helmet she wore kept the wind off her face, it was still an exhilirating experience to weave through the streets of Tokyo.

Just up ahead, the AR-HUD highlighted Miyata's building. She pulled up in front of the tower and looked up. The AR-HUD projected an arrow on the tenth floor and pulled out a separate layout of just that level, highlighting Miyata's unit. She climbed off the cycle and removed the helmet, setting it in a stand that emerged from the front console.

The front door had biometric security, so just as she had done when she paid Takahashi a visit, Erika activated her armor's nanites. They flowed over her hand and she placed it on the scanner to override the settings. She then did the same for the elevator and took it up to Miyata's floor.

Once inside his condo—or what used to be his condo, at least—Erika began moving through. It was a large place with a kitchen and dining area that greeted her just past the main hallway. The condo looked like it was a newer construction. Units like this went for quite a bit of money, and as one of the best engineers at the top tech company in the nation, Miyata would have had the means to afford it.

Past the kitchen was a living room with a large flat-panel TV screen mounted on the wall. There were shelves that held framed photographs. Erika took one of them and looked at it. The photo was of Miyata, but he looked at least ten years younger. There was a woman the same age and he had his arm around her, smiles on both their faces. Another framed photograph featured two children—both girls. But one had white skin and green eyes with red hair. The other was black, with dark curls and large brown eyes.

She set the photo back down and looked through more. The same woman and children appeared in many of the framed pictures Miyata had on display. As she continued to look through them, she ran a search on the files Adachi had provided her with.

The search took no time at all, and there was no record of Miyata ever being married. Nor did his name appear on any adoption records. So who were these people? A lost love? A friend's children?

She opened a call back to HQ. After a few moments, she heard Adachi's voice in her ear, sounding annoyed at having been disturbed. She didn't care, Tokkei cases always took priority, so he would have no choice but to do what she wanted.

"It's Agent Kuroki," she said.

"Yes, I see that from the caller ID. What may I do for you, Agent Kuroki?"

"I need a facial recognition search."

He sighed. "Fine, awaiting upload."

She focused on the photograph of the woman. Her AR-HUD opened a separate window that zoomed in close on the woman's face and Erika snapped the photo. She then did the same thing with the two girls.

"The photos seem about ten years old or so."

"That's no problem for us. I'll call you back when I have some results."

The line went dead and Erika continued her search. He was a prickly sort and it was clear he didn't like having to run errands for the Tokkei. But he also knew he had no choice, so Erika didn't bother worrying too much over his misgivings.

From the living room she checked the bedroom next. There were some other photographs here. She opened his closet and saw several empty hangers. That led her to backtrack to the bathroom. The clothes hamper and washing machine were both empty. At the bathroom sink, she opened the medicine cabinet, where she saw a tooth-bruth rack without a single toothbrush. Erika returned to the kitchen and opened the refrigerator. Inside were just a few random items—a couple cans of beer, a bottle of mayonnaise, a jar of mustard, and half a head of garlic. No vegetables of any kind. The freezer was completely empty.

Two possibilities started to form in Erika's mind. The first was that Miyata had been taken by some very generous kidnappers who gave him time to pack up his things and clean out his refrigerator. That seemed unlikely, so it left the second option—not only did he run off, but he'd bee planning to. Which leant more credence to Hiro's theory that he was behind the stolen technology.

Her AR-HUD signaled an incoming call from Adachi and she activated it. "Kuroki here."

"Hello, Agent. I ran the trace. Nothing on the two *gaijin.*"

"And the woman?"

"One possible match—Keiko Izumi."

"Okay, and where can I find her?"

"You can't," said Adachi. "It seems Keiko Izumi died five years ago."

"She's dead?" asked Erika.

"Yes, I'm fairly certain that's what I said," said Adachi, the condescension clear in his voice.

"What was the cause of death?" asked Erika, trying to ignore his tone.

"Suicide," said Adachi. "Pills."

So much for that lead, she thought.

"Where did she die?" asked Erika.

"At a hotel in Shinjuku."

"Did she have any family?"

"The file shows nothing."

"Okay, thank you."

Now it was her turn to cut the line abruptly. She wondered what it was about Adachi that set her so on edge. Was it just his condescension, or was it the way he had said the word *gaijin*? She'd heard it used as an insult so often when she was a child. Even though she was *hafu* or mixed, that didn't matter to the other kids. And since then, she'd heard it so often in the Jietai that she'd become used to it. Yet somehow, when Adachi had used it just then about those two girls, it gnawed at her.

There was one room left. The apartment was a two-bedroom and Miyata had used the second bedroom as a home office. She sat at the glass desk and activated the computer. The plastic screen displayed a login window. Erika activated her nanites and they spread over her face, partially forming the goggles of her mask. Just enough to fool the retinal scanner.

"Access denied," said the computer as the words flashed on the screen. "Would you like to try again?"

She did so, but the result was the same. Normally it would seem unreal for Tokkei tech to be incapable of overriding a simple computer login. But this computer had belonged to one of Yoshida's best and brightest, so perhaps it wasn't so far-fetched after all.

Erika examined the computer unit itself. It was a small, white box, no larger than her hand. She unplugged the power cord and the login screen vanished from the flat glass monitor. Erika would take it back to Adachi and have him examine it for some idea of what it meant. Until then, she had one more place to visit—Yoshida Technologies, where Miyata had worked.

浪人

The main office for Yoshida Technologies was located

in the Shibuya ward, just a few minutes by hovercycle from Miyata's building in Aoyama. Erika had hoped she might get another call from Adachi informing her of some new information discovered about Keiko Izumi or the two foreign girls, but her comms were silent.

Yoshida Tech was the owner and sole occupant of the tallest skyscraper in Shibuya. She had never been inside, but she knew from the Tokkei's files that there were several floors devoted not only to corporate activities, but also research and development.

She drove the bike into the underground parking garage and found a space for other cycles. Erika powered it down and the bike gently rested itself on bumpers that ran around the bottom rim of the antigravity unit.

There were no buttons in the elevator, just a touchpad. A message was written on a sign above the pad, instructing all guests to go through the lobby first. Erika placed her hand on the pad and when asked for the floor, she said, "Lobby."

The doors opened to the lobby, revealing a bustle of activity with people in suits moving back and forth from the elevator bay and the front entrance. Near the entrance was a reception counter, and she went up to it to see a dark-skinned man in a security uniform.

"Can I help you?" he asked. His Japanese was heavily accented, though Erika couldn't quite determine where he was from.

She reached into her pocket and took out a badge, then showed it to the security guard. "My name is Erika Kuroki, I'm a Tokkei agent and I need to speak with someone regarding Kenjiro Miyata."

The guard studied the badge for a few seconds and then

nodded his understanding as he picked up a phone. "Just one moment please."

Erika looked away from the guard as he made the call. She studied the faces of the Yoshida employees as they moved about. There were a mix of nationalities here, and Yoshida had prided itself on its ability to attract top talent from all over the world. It seemed all the more ironic that their pirated technology was now being tested on refugees. Even more ironic that one of their best engineers was apparently behind it.

"Agent," said the guard, drawing her attention back to him. "An escort will be down here shortly to take you where you need to go."

"Thank you," she said.

Fortunately for Erika, a Tokkei badge meant the wait was short. Soon, she heard someone call her name and she turned around. A white man with short, brown hair and glasses stood before her dressed in a suit. He took out a business card and held it with both hands, then bowed and offered it to her.

"My name is Gardner Takasu, I've been asked to answer any questions you have about Dr. Miyata."

Erika bowed and accepted the card. She then did the same with her own business card.

Gardner instructed her to follow him and he led her into the elevator bay. He placed his hand on the pad and when asked what floor, his response was, "Conference center."

Erika wasn't sure why he was taking her there instead of the research and development section, but she supposed he had his reasons. For now, she would simply follow his lead. She studied his card and noticed that his title was

"VICE-PRESIDENT OF GOVERNMENT RELA-TIONS."

"Takasu is an interesting family name, given your face," she said.

"My biological parents were killed in the Second American Civil War when I was five," said Gardner. "I was adopted."

"I'm sorry," said Erika, immediately regretting having brought up his name at all.

Gardner offered her a smile. "Don't be. It was so long ago, I don't even remember them. Or even living anywhere other than Tokyo. The Takasus have been very generous to me throughout my life. As far as I'm concerned, they are my real parents."

The elevator stopped and the AI announced they had arrived at the conference center. Gardner led Erika out the elevator and into a conference room with translucent walls. Once they were inside, he said, "Enable privacy mode."

The lights brightened and the walls tinted. He gestured for Erika to have a seat at the round table and she did, then he sat across from her at the other end.

"I'm curious why you brought me here, Mr. Takasu," said Erika. "As I said, I'm interested in learning more about Dr. Miyata's disappearance."

"Yes, I'm aware. And I've already been informed by the Ministry that you would be coming down."

"Informed by whom?"

"Your superior officer, of course. Agent Yoshida," said Gardner. "I spoke to him personally. He said you were likely to come and ask questions about Dr. Miyata. I took the liberty of making your job a little easier."

He reached into his jacket and held up a small data

diskette for her to see, then tossed it across the table. Erika caught it with ease and held it in her hand, her implants reading the data.

"That diskette contains Miyata's full employment record here at Yoshida Technologies. Every bit of information we have on him is listed in there."

Erika's implants processed the data and she issued a silent command to run a quick search. There was the possibility something could be missed, but she had to check anyway. When no results were returned, she looked Gardner in the eyes.

"Do you know the name Keiko Izumi?"

Gardner hesitated for a moment and then asked, "I'm sorry, who?"

"Keiko Izumi. She committed suicide five years ago."

"I…don't believe I've ever heard of anyone by that name. Why?"

"There were photos of her and Miyata together in his apartment. Also photos of two unidentified non-Japanese girls."

"I really have no clue what you're talking about, Agent," said Gardner.

"Did you know Miyata? Personally, I mean."

"We were in different departments, of course. But with my position, I've often had to prepare presentations to the government on different technologies in development. So I had some occasions to speak with him."

"And what was he like?"

Gardner took a breath and looked up as he searched his memories. Erika studied his facial features carefully, watching for any strange behavior, and she instructed her AR-HUD to present any discrepencies in his expressions.

"He was…unremarkable, to be honest. Not in terms of his intellect—in that, he was definitely a genius," said Gardner. "But I mean when it came to dealing with others. Not exactly what you might call a people person."

"I see," said Erika. "And you're certain you know nothing about any involvement he had with Keiko Izumi? Or any children he may have adopted?"

"He didn't seem the type to get involved with anyone. I doubt the man had much of a social life," said Gardner. "And as for children, that seems even less likely."

The analysis showed nothing unusual in Gardner's reactions to the questions, nor in his responses. Erika had to conclude that he was telling the truth—or at least he believed he was.

She would have to go through the records Gardner provided her with. But even then, it didn't seem likely that anything would turn up that might be of any use.

"These records, do they include details about the projects Miyata was working on?" asked Erika.

"There are references to them. Though of course you understand that some of the sensitive details have been redacted," said Gardner.

Erika raised an eyebrow. "You're redacting sensitive details from a Tokkei agent?"

"For the time being," said Gardner. "Our unique relationship with the Ministry of Defense grants us some privileges that wouldn't otherwise be available to other companies. However, if there is something you require more details on, I suggest you tell Agent Yoshida what you need to see and the reason for it. He will handle it from there."

"I see," said Erika, wondering just how normal this

kind of relationship really was, and wondering just what Gardner and Yoshida Tech might want to keep hidden, even from the Tokkei.

"Those photos…of that woman and the girls…you said you found them in Dr. Miyata's apartment?" asked Gardner.

Erika nodded.

"I don't suppose you found anything else of interest…?"

Erika paused and waited for him to give an example. When Gardner provided none, she prompted him: "Such as…?"

Gardner sighed. "Such as a computer? Or any data storage?"

She had found the computer, though she wanted to keep that to herself for the time being. If Yoshida Tech was already keeping things from her, she wondered if they would try to look at the computer's data before she had a chance to.

"I'm sorry, but no," said Erika. "If he had any data storage in his apartment, he must have taken them with him when he left."

"Hmm…that's a shame," said Gardner. "Something like that may have provided some explanation of where he went or what exactly he was mixed up in."

"I agree. But the records you've provided will be a big help, I'm sure." Erika stood and bowed. "Thank you for your valuable time, Mr. Takasu."

Gardner stood and bowed himself. "It was my pleasure, Agent Kuroki. And if there is anything else I or Yoshida Technologies can do to assist in your investigation, please do not hesitate to contact me."

"I will," said Erika, and then he escorted her back to the elevator.

Erika rode the elevator down to the parking garage alone. She couldn't help the little chuckle that jumped out from her mouth. If not for that encounter, she may not have suspected anything strange involving Yoshida. But Gardner's performance made her think they did indeed have something to hide.

Now the question was what.

CHAPTER 15

As soon as Erika left the parking garage and pulled onto the main road, she got the sense that she was being followed. She glanced at the display on the hovercycle's dashboard, which provided a view from behind via camera.

It was likely she was simply being paranoid. But she didn't want to dismiss anything without first checking it out. She took a turn at the next corner and continued glancing at the display. Another rider turned the corner as well. She took another few turns and each time, the rider continued to follow her.

Erika accelerated the hovercycle, trying to put some more distance between her and the rider. She began to weave in and out of the lanes. The rider continued to try to keep pace with her and there was no doubt in her mind that this was a definite tail.

A ramp was just ahead, leading to one of the expressways. Erika sped up the ramp and merged into the highway traffic. The rider seemed to have broken off, probably because they realized they'd been spotted and it was useless to continue trying.

Erika smiled to herself beneath her helmet as she passed an exit. She'd get off at the next one, then loop around and return to HQ. She did wonder who exactly would be tailing her in the first place, though, briefly wondering if maybe Gardner had put someone on her just in case.

She checked the display and then she noticed there was a new rider a few cars behind. Definitely different from the first, and now Erika was getting extremely suspicious. It wasn't just one person, now it seemed a group was tailing her.

"The hell is going on…?" she muttered to herself.

Erika decided the time was right to confront her pursuer. She reduced her speed and allowed the rider to catch up to her. The next exit was just ahead and Erika took a hard turn to take the off-ramp.

The rider almost missed the exit, but did follow. Erika merged into the street traffic. There was an interection just ahead with the light turning from yellow to red. She throttled up and blew through the red light. Cars from oncoming traffic swerved and honked, colliding and creating a pile-up. The rider accelerated themselves and boosted, flying over the accident.

Erika pulled a hard left at the next corner, running another red light and making some of the cars slide to avoid her. More turns followed and the chase continued. The rider was good and she had to admit that a part of her was enjoying the chase. Still, it was time to bring this to an end.

They were getting away from the populated areas. Now they were in the nightlife district, which was pretty much dead at this time of day. Erika turned down one of the small streets and swerved to a stop. All around her were bars and clubs, closed for business until the sun went down. It was like a ghost town.

The rider turned the corner and remained at the end of the street, staring at Erika. She climbed off her hovercycle and removed her helmet. The rider didn't do the same, just remained on their cycle.

Erika heard something and glanced over her shoulder. At the other end of the street was the first rider. Judging from the body types she could now see, both appeared to be men.

They revved their cycles and Erika readied herself for what was going to come next. Both took off, racing at her from the opposite ends of the street. Erika tapped the container on her wrist to release the nanites. They covered her body within seconds as she leapt at the rider who had been following her the most.

Her kick took the rider off his vehicle and the cycle spun out. The other rider managed to avoid it and raced for Erika. She extended her sword and jumped as the rider came at her, using the energy blade to slice through the front of the cycle.

Erika turned to face the two riders, raising her sword. The two got to their feet and drew handguns, quickly opening fire. She dodged many rounds, and sliced through others. As soon as the guns clicked on empty, Erika charged.

She changed the setting on her sword. Whoever these two were, she wanted to find out exactly why they followed and then attacked her, and dead men weren't very responsive to questioning. She plunged the energy blade into one of the riders, and he screamed from behind his helmet before collapsing.

Taking out one gave the other an opportunity to reload and start firing again. Erika's armor protected her from the rounds and she reached out with her free hand. Her fingers wrapped around the gun's barrel and when she squeezed, the strength provided by her armor enabled her to crush the weapon. She then grabbed the rider by the throat and drove her blade into his chest.

The two men were both lying on the ground, moaning in pain from the synaptic shock caused by the sword. Erika retracted the blade and knelt down by one, pulling off his helmet.

"Who are you?" she asked. "Why are you following me?"

"Go to hell…" he muttered.

Erika smacked him with his own helmet. He let out a cry of pain in response.

"Wrong answer," she said. "Now are you going to tell me what I want to know or should I hit you again?"

"Fuck off, fascist."

She struck him two more times with his helmet and both times he gave a shout of pain. His nose was now bloodied and welts were forming on his face.

"Keep it up. I've literally got all day," she said.

"Stop!" called out the other rider, lying on his stomach and reaching a hand out. "We were just hired to do a job, that's it!"

"Someone hired you to kill a Tokkei agent?" she asked.

"The computer. We were sent to get it, but you got there before us," he continued.

Gardner had mentioned Miyata's computer, too. Apparently there was something on it that was important. Now it seemed likely that he was responsible for sending these two braintrusts after her.

"Were you sent by a white guy named Takasu?" she asked.

"We're not telling you!" said the bloodied rider. Erika struck him again.

"Shut up, Shin!" said the second rider.

"You don't have to listen to him, Shin. I kind of enjoy hitting you," said Erika.

"'Cause you're a fascist bitch, that's why!"

She hit him again. "See? It gets funnier every time."

"We don't know!" said the second one.

Erika moved from Shin over to the more talkative one. "What are you called?"

He sighed. "Jo. Just leave Shin be, he's an idiot and he'll let you kill him before he talks."

"Save his life and tell me about this man," said Erika.

"All I know is he gave us the means to get into the apartment and told us to find his computer. But when we got there, we saw you come out. Shin tailed you to Shibuya just in case you had taken it. Once I confirmed it was gone, we figured you had to have it, so we both came after you."

"Okay, Jo, how much did this guy pay you? How much does it take for you to risk a charge of attempted murder of a Tokkei agent?"

"A hundred grand."

"One hundred thousand yen? That's it?"

"Times are tough," said Shin. "Not a lot we can do about it."

"That's pretty pathetic, even for thugs like you," said Erika. "So if this guy wanted you to steal the computer, obviously he'd need a rendezvous point."

"We were supposed to call him once we had it, then set up the meet."

"Good, do it," said Erika. "Tell him you have the computer and you're ready to get paid."

"And then what's gonna happen to us?" asked Jo.

"Maybe if you help me out, I say you were useful to the investigation and you get a break," said Erika. "Or I can arrest you both now and have you thrown in a hole for the rest of your miserable lives."

"Don't do it, Jo!" said Shin, which earned another blow from Erika.

"Make the call, Jo. Give me a hand here and I promise I won't hold your friend's stupidity against him," said Erika.

Jo sighed and nodded. "Okay, I'll do it."

"Good, get on with it." Erika stood and made a call on her own to HQ. "Kuroki here. I need transport for two arrests. Sending you coordinates now."

If it was indeed Gardner who sent these two after her, he'd be in a lot of trouble. But then Erika also wondered if it could be Miyata himself who hired them. Only one of the two seemed likely, which meant whatever Miyata had on his computer had to be very important.

CHAPTER 16

The small room at HQ that Erika stood in was sandwiched between two interrogation rooms. There was a two-way window on each of the walls, and she looked back and forth to each. The room to the left was where Jo waited and the right housed Shin. They both looked nervous as they waited for what would come next.

There was a knock on the door followed by it opening. Hiro stepped inside and approached her, then turned on the holographic projector on his gauntlet—the only part of his armor that was active. There were two holograms displayed, both of them mugshots matching the two prisoners.

"We've got Jotaro Iida and Shinya Omi," said Hiro. "Both are twenty, and both have in and out of juvenile detention since the age of twelve. Bosozoku orphans."

The bosozoku were biker gangs. For a time, their kind seemed to have died out. But over the course of the past two decades or so, they'd seen a resurgence. Most of their recruits came from the dregs of society—orphans, the poor, illegal immigrants, runaways. The people who had no real future.

"Did you bring in Takasu for questioning?" she asked.

Hiro scoffed. "Are you crazy?"

Erika did a double-take. "Am I missing something? What's crazy about it?"

"You want me to march into Yoshida Tech—the corporation that the Ministry of Defense is pretty much dependent on—and arrest their VP of government relations?" His neck bent forward. "And you *don't* see why that's crazy?"

"As soon as I walked out of there, these two punks show up looking for *the exact same thing* Takasu asked me about. And *you* don't think that's suspicious?"

Hiro exhaled a long breath. "Did either of these bastards mention Takasu by name?"

"No, but—"

"Did they give a description of him?"

"They didn't deal face-to-face. The arrangements were all made online."

Hiro shrugged. "Then you've got nothing. Just wild speculation. We can't arrest someone based only on your word." He turned back to the door. "Let's give them some time to stew and then we can try questioning them."

"Would you be this concerned about evidence if Takasu wasn't working for Yoshida?"

Hiro's shoulders stiffened. As soon as the words escaped Erika's lips, she knew they were a mistake. He turned, his gaze hardened as he stepped closer to her. His voice was low but his tone was biting.

"Are you insinuating that I'm looking the other way because we're dealing with my family's company?"

"I'm sorry, sir. I was just…"

"Maybe you'd like to speak to the general about your idea? See if he feels the same way?" Hiro reached a hand for his ear as if he were about to make the call. "I can call him up right now. Sure, he's in a meeting with the Prime Minister, but I'm sure he'd make an exception for you, right?"

Erika looked down at the floor. "I apologize, Agent Yoshida. My comment was out of line."

"Damn straight it was."

They were both silent for a few beats. Hiro's hard expression softened before he spoke again.

"What about this computer everyone seems to be looking for?" he asked. "Did you find it at Miyata's condo?"

The smart thing to do would be to bring Hiro completely in on this, to tell him that yes, she did indeed find a computer at Miyata's home, but she couldn't break into it. But Hiro's reluctance to investigate Gardner triggered something in her. It was the same feeling she had when Hiro told her to drop the Kitano investigation. And so with all that swirling around her mind, she surprised herself with the next words that came out of her mouth.

"No, there was nothing there."

"Hmm, that's a shame," said Hiro. "If we had access to the data on it, we might know just why Takasu and these two yahoos were so keen on getting their hands on it."

Erika just went on instinct when she told Hiro she didn't find the computer, but now she saw a potential problem. She already knew the encryption was too strong for her armor's systems, and she couldn't very well ask Adachi for help. He would certainly reach out to Hiro and then Hiro would know she lied.

"Have you seen my report about Keiko Izumi and

those girls?" asked Erika.

Hiro nodded. "Yeah, we're trying to find out more information about Izumi, trying to figure out exactly how Miyata might have known her. And as for those girls, we've sent the photos out to the Immigration Services Agency and the Orphanage Association and asked them to cross-check them against their records. But even then, there's no guarantee anything will turn up. If those girls were in the country illegally, we may not be able to find any records on them."

"It makes you wonder," said Erika. "That poor soul we fought under Kitano's place, he was also a 'non-entity' in the eyes of the system."

"You suggesting there's a connection? Maybe Miyata was using these girls as test subjects, too?"

"They certainly didn't seem that way in the photos I saw. In fact, it seemed Miyata cared for them."

"It's more than likely a dead end anyway, so I wouldn't worry too much about it," said Hiro. "What do you say we leave these bastards danging on the hook for a while, get in a sparring session, and then come back and question them?"

Erika stared at Jo through the two-way mirror. Then she looked at Hiro and gave a tiny smile as she shook her head. "Thanks, but I think I'll pass. Takasu gave me some files detailing Miyata's history with the company, so I think it'd be better if I go through that stuff first. And there's quite a lot in there."

"Suit yourself. I'll come back in about two hours and we can question them then."

Hiro left with that, but Erika remained in the room, her gaze still trained on Jo. While they waited for the prisoner transport to arrive, he'd reached out to his contact, but there was no answer. Erika checked her pocket. The small phone was still in there. Most people communicated with implants these days, but there were those who couldn't or didn't want to. In some cases, it was a simple matter of financial difficulty.

But that wasn't always the case. Legal implants were registered to the host's genetic markers, which made tracking calls very easy. That meant there was a very large market for untraceable phones.

She took the device out of her pocket and turned it on. There was an unread text message from a blocked number. Erika opened it. Jo's initial message—which he sent in her presence—told the buyer they'd found the 'book.' She knew that at least was a reference to the computer.

"Is it the latest edition?" was the response sent by the buyer.

Erika stepped outside the room and looked around. There was no one else here and so she went into the interrogation room. Fortunately there were no cameras in here in order to give the Ministry of Defense deniability if any allegations of prisoner abuse were ever raised against the Tokkei.

She walked up to the table and set the phone down in front of Jo. He looked at the message and then up at her.

"I need to know everything about this code your buyer's using," said Erika.

"He asked if it's the latest edition. 'Yes' means we got in and out clean. 'No' means there was someone else. If it's a first edition, that means we ran into some problems, but we managed to get away with it. Say it's a second edition, that means they didn't see us, but we saw them."

"Okay," said Erika. "Tell him it's a secnd edition."

"You sure?"

"Did I stutter?"

Jo sighed and typed out the reply. Erika didn't want to make it seem like it was too easy. Whoever this was seemed smart, and would probably expect some other people were also interested in the computer.

"Got a reply," said Jo. "Asking about the quality. Good condition means the other people after it were cops or government types. Poor means it was his company. Decent means we don't know who they were."

"Decent," said Erika.

Again, Jo typed in the response. And once more, the response came almost immediately.

"He said he'll contact soon with more details about where to meet."

"Good." Erika took the phone back and put it in her pocket. She went to the door and just when she was about to open it, she looked back at Jo. "Listen, you're going to be interrogated in a few hours. If you mention anything about our deal or this conversation, you're going to *wish* you ended up in a blacksite."

Jo swallowed hard and nodded. "Okay, I gotcha. No problem."

Erika left the room. These two were just regular street toughs and they didn't know much. Hiro wouldn't have a reason to lean on them as hard as he did Kitano, so she doubted she'd have anything to worry about.

But there was still the issue about the computer. She needed to find a way to read the data on there and determine just what it said about Miyata. She had a hunch it would lead her to the next clue in this investigation, but for some reason she didn't trust the Tokkei to keep her in the loop about this.

Erika boarded the elevator for the Tokkei office. As she rode the elevator up from the detention level, she sent a message, asking to meet in the conference room. After a moment, a response came.

"Why?"

"There's something we have to talk about," she wrote back. *"It's not what you think. Honest."*

Erika waited for the next response to come through on her AR-HUD. The elevator reached the floor and she hesitated before stepping off. Then finally, it came: *"Okay, which one?"*

She sighed with relief and left the elevator. Erika found an empty conference room and walked inside. She sent him the number and then sat at the long conference table, just waiting.

A few moments later, there was a knock on the door and it opened. Masao stood on the other side of the door and he peeked in with some apprehension.

"Come in," she said.

He entered, looking sheepish. She almost wanted to laugh at the way this big, tough guy acted like a junior high schooler trying to approach a girl for the first time.

"Listen, Kuroki…about last night…" he began.

She held up her hand. "Masao, I didn't ask you here to talk about that. I'm being serious here. But there *is* something I need your help with."

"Oh?" he asked. "What, is this like…a case?"

She paused before saying, "…something like that."

Masao's brows were arched in confusion. "Don't think I really follow…"

She sighed, knowing this would be difficult to talk about. "Okay, listen. Say…I needed to break into some encrypted files…"

"You'd talk to cyber, obviously."

"What if I couldn't?" she asked.

Masao raised his head and looked down at her through narrowed eyelids. "And…why couldn't you go to cyber…?"

"Just…" she huffed. "It's a sensitive issue, okay? And I don't know who can be trusted with it. There might be some corruption angles to this."

Masao sighed and turned, going for the door. Erika jumped from her chair and onto the table. She ran across, the nanites swarming over her body. She flipped off the table and landed right in front of Masao. He gasped and backed off a few steps as her helmet nanites receded to reveal her face.

"Kuroki, I dunno what's goin' on here, but—"

"Please, I just need you to trust me," said Erika. "If you needed to go to someone to break an encryption—and we're talking encryption too strong for our armor—who would it be?"

Masao took a deep breath and thought about it. He went to the door and opened it just a crack to look down both ends of the hallway, then closed it again.

"Midnight," he said. "There's a basement bar in Roppongi called Karasu. Don't tell anyone you're going."

"Thank you," she said, and then added, "…Masao."

"Don't be late." Masao left the room and closed the door behind him.

CHAPTER 17

The minutes and hours seemed to drag as Erika waited for the opportunity to advance her investigation. She'd gone through the motions of the rest of the day, reading through Yoshida's records on Miyata. But just as she had assumed, there was nothing in there that really told her anything useful.

And there were indeed a lot of redactions on the projects he was involved with. Gardner had told her she had the option of going through Hiro to see about getting more details on those projects, but she didn't feel like it would be worth the effort. Gardner would find a way to stall and slow-walk the process. And since Hiro's family owned the company, he wouldn't be willing to push back against them too hard.

But if Masao had someone who could get into Miyata's computer, that seemed like the better path. And then, if it turned out the computer proved useful, how would Erika explain it? How could she explain why she didn't go to cyber to have them try it or why she lied about even having the computer? That was a question for another time. She couldn't dwell on it now.

After she left the office, she had a quick dinner at a ramen stand, then returned home and just waited. But she felt restless the whole time. Trying to find ways to kill time before she had to head to Roppongi just made her even more anxious.

When it was time to go, Erika left her armor behind, but she took a small bag with the computer inside. After Hiro proved he could track the armor, she didn't want to risk that the Tokkei may have been monitoring her movements. Roppongi was in her ward and she could get there on foot.

It was just before eleven-thirty when she left her apartment, and that gave her time to reach the bar in Roppongi. There was a chill in the air and she pulled up the hood of her windbreaker. She could see the environment beginning to shift as she moved from one neighborhood to the next. There was a decrease in the newer apartment buildings and an increase in older, more dilapidated ones. The restaurants and bars became dingier and less flashy.

She was now in the midst of a web-like pattern of narrow streets stretching throughout the entertainment district. Off on the outskirts was an old, six-story building. The signs advertising each floor were not lit up and sometimes broken. And there was a staircase leading down into a darkened area with a dim, red light. Erika descended the steps and saw a solid door with KARASU scrawled over the front. She reached for the door and opened it.

It was a narrow establishment with a high counter. There were no stools and there was just enough room to stand in front of the bar. A young black man stood behind the bar and looked at her.

"What are you drinking?" he asked.

"Beer is fine," said Erika as she moved in front of the counter.

"We don't have a tap, just bottles."

"That's fine, just give me whatever you've got."

The bartender nodded and turned around to retrieve a bottle of Asahi from a refrigerator behind him. He removed the cap and set the bottle on the counter in front of her. Erika picked up the bottle and started sipping the drink. She stared at the entrance out of the corner of her eye and wondered just when Masao was going to get here.

"Don't see many girls like you in here," said the bartender. "Mostly it's just roughnecks."

"I'm meeting a friend."

"What's your name? I'm James."

Erika looked at him with a sigh. "Listen, James. I don't mean to be rude but I'm really not up for small talk. I know you're just trying to do your job, but I'd prefer waiting in silence."

"Fair enough," said James. "Sorry to bother you."

"Nothing personal," she said.

Erika finished the first beer and ordered another. She checked the time and saw it was almost quarter after midnight. Finally, the door opened and she looked towards the source. The man who entered had the same large frame as Masao and he wore a baseball cap with the brim pulled down low. James didn't even wait for him to ask for a drink, just produced another Asahi from the refrigerator and put it down in front of him.

Silence lingered in the air. James looked down at his

phone and said, "I've gotta make a call. I'll be back in a few minutes."

He left the bar and Erika heard his footsteps going up the stairs. Once the sound was gone, the man took off his hat.

"Sorry about the cloak-and-dagger routine," he said. "You never know who's watching."

"Never pegged you for the paranoid type," said Erika.

"I grew up in a rough neighborhood. Jietai was my ticket out, but I've still got friends."

"James?" she asked.

"He's a good guy, we grew up together. Knows how to connect you with just about anyone you might need," said Masao. "Well…you know…the extra-legal stuff, that is."

"You could probably earn yourself a nice little commendation if you took him down," said Erika.

"Oh no doubt. And if I did that, then not only would I be sacrificing a valuable source for times like this, but I'd also be screwing over someone who's like a brother to me."

"Not the kind of talk you'd expect from a Tokkei agent," said Erika.

"You grow up the way we did, you don't got the luxury of racism," said Masao.

They heard footsteps again and Masao put his cap back on. The door opened and a young woman entered with James behind her. Her hair was cut short and stylized in the form of pink spikes. She came into the bar and stood between Erika and Masao. James served her a beer and then left once more.

"Erika Kuroki, born in Osaka," said the woman as she took a sip of her beer. "Mother, Mako Kuroki. Father, Adam Kim. Korean descent, born in America, emigrated to

Japan as a university student."

"You seem to know a lot about me," said Erika.

"Parents divorced when you were nine years old. Your mother took you to her hometown in Shizuoka. She worked as a secretary, struggling to make ends meet. Eventually, you joined the Jietai." She looked at Erika. "Why did you join? You wanted citizenship status? An education? Or do you believe in the cause?"

"What does it matter?" asked Erika.

"Because the reasons say a lot about you."

"You know a lot about me, but I don't know a thing about you," said Erika.

"That's because I work very hard to keep it that way." She took a swig of her beer. "Call me Himiko."

"That your given name?"

"The one I gave myself," said Himiko. "So you gonna answer the question or what?"

It had been some time since Erika had thought about her reasons for joining the Jietai. But she had never forgotten them.

"Money," she said. "Like you said, my mother struggled to make ends meet. I wanted to make sure she could retire."

"How'd that work out?"

Erika looked down at the bottle and started picking at the label. She felt the emotion deep in her gut, but she'd learned over the years how to suppress it. She took a deep breath and steeled herself, then took a sip.

"She died while I was stationed overseas," said Erika.

"And your father?"

"He was killed at a protest rally."

"You've been honest with me," said Himiko. "I like that."

"Can you help me out?"

Himiko finished off the rest of the beer and moved from the counter. "Come with me. Stay a few steps behind."

Erika looked at Masao and he nodded. She took a final sip and then followed Himiko out the bar. Himiko was already crossing the street once Erika reached the top of the steps.

She followed, with Himiko leading her down a series of side-streets, taking turns that seemed random. Erika saw Himiko go into a dilapidated building, maybe seven stories. She climbed the stairs behind Himiko, all the way up to the top floor. Once they reached the top, Himiko unlocked the door and stepped inside first.

Himiko turned on the lights and Erika was a little surprised at what she saw. It seemed like this had once been a hostess bar and there were even booths and couch still lining the walls and a bar. But what was more amazing were the changes Himiko had made to the place. There was a desk and once Himiko had turned on the lights, about a dozen holographic displays flipped up on the plastic panels.

Erika was impressed by the system she had set up here. "How did you end up here?"

"My mom used to own this place," said Himiko. "Left it to me after she died. But I wasn't willing to run a hostess bar. Plus, most other businesses had gone out by that point, so I decided to set this up as my place."

Himiko turned and fixed her gaze on Erika. "Now let's be clear about something, okay? Masao's an old friend, so I'm just doing this as a favor to him. And I've got cameras recording us right now, so if any of those Tokkei guys come after me, I've got material on you."

"You seem paranoid," said Erika.

"That's why I'm still alive," said Himiko. "Masao said something about a computer you need to get into?"

Erika took the small computer unit out of her bag and handed it to Himiko. She took the casing and examined it from every angle.

"That's interesting…" she muttered.

"What is?" asked Erika.

"It's got ports."

"And?"

"Most devices these days use wireless data transmission, so many don't even have ports anymore. But this does, so you'd need to physically connect storage devices to transfer data."

"Still not sure I follow," said Erika.

"No matter how secure your device may be, no matter how well-encrypted your data, if you're transmitting wirelessly, there's a risk it could be intercepted. That goes for both peripherals and transferring data," said Himiko. "The ports suggest whoever had this computer intended to stick to more secure transmission."

That backed up her encounter with the bosozoku and Gardner. Whatever Miyata had on this computer was no doubt very sensitive. And she wanted to know what it was.

Himiko went off and came back a few moments later with a physical keyboard. She plugged the cable into one of the ports and booted up the computer. Himiko bypassed the regular boot-up procedure and went into the command line. Her fingers danced around the keyboard as she typed in line after line of code. The letters moved too fast for Erika to even follow.

"Any idea how long this will take?" asked Erika.

"A long time," said Himiko. "I've got to bypass the

biometric login and have to go through a bunch of code in order to do it. So fix yourself a drink and get comfortable."

Erika sighed and went behind the bar. There were some bottles in the bar well and glasses under the counter. She grabbed an empty glass and then took a bottle of rum from the well and filled the glass.

"Hey Kuroki," said Himiko. "While you're behind there, get me a Jack on the rocks."

She rolled her eyes, but complied. Himiko might have been a bit gruff, but she seemed to know what she was doing. And that was what Erika was counting on to move forward with this.

A vibration in her pocket distracted her while preparing Himiko's drink. Erika reached into her pocket to draw out the phone she took from Jo. There was a new text message from a blocked number. Erika brought up the message.

"Tomorrow morning. Seven AM. Ueno Park."

Erika stared at the phone, unsure of what to respond with. The only sound in the room was the clatter of the keyboards as Himiko tried to bypass the security protocols.

"You said this will take a long time," said Erika. "Any chance that it would be finished by seven?"

Himiko's fingers stopped hitting the keys and looked over her shoulder. "By *seven*?"

Erika nodded.

"Kuroki, that's…that's like, just over six hours from now."

"Is there a chance?"

"No! *Fuck* no!" protested Himiko. "Even if I can get into the computer, whatever files you need on here are no doubt encrypted. I have to run a program to decrypt those and I have no way of telling how long that would take."

Erika sighed and raised the glass of rum to her lips. "Dammit."

"Why would you need it that soon anyway?" asked Himiko.

Erika set her glass down. She moved from behind the bar, Himiko's drink in one hand and the phone in the other. Once Erika reached the desk, she held out both for Himiko. The young hacker accepted both and read the text message.

"Who's this?" she asked.

"Whoever's after this thing," said Erika. "Might be my chance at finding out just what's going on. And if I knew just what was on it, I'd have leverage going into this meeting."

"Could also be a trap," said Himiko.

"They think I'm the guy who stole it for them, so I don't think so."

"Could *still* be a trap. Maybe they'd planned to kill the errand boy once the errand was done."

Himiko had a good point. Erika had no way of knowing just what she was walking into. But she also couldn't miss this opportunity to learn more about what this was all about. She had to take some kind of action here.

"You're doing this as a favor to Ishiyama, that I get," said Erika. "But if I asked you for something, what would you charge?"

Himiko raised an eyebrow. "Depends on what you need."

CHAPTER 18

Ueno Park was very large and one of the few natural landscapes still left in Tokyo. It contained numerous footpaths, temples, shrines, and even museums. Erika had never even been here before. She'd only recently come to Tokyo when she was promoted to the Tokkei and didn't have much time for sight-seeing.

Now she walked over the paths, a cup of hot coffee in her hand. Her implants were active with an open line of communication with Himiko back in Roppongi.

"How's it looking?" asked Erika.

"Wired up. I've tapped into the park's surveillance system, so I've got eyes all over Ueno," said Himiko through Erika's implants. "It's a big place. You got a more specific meeting area?"

"Yeah, got a text while I was on the train," said Erika, checking the phone. "The Saigo Takamori statue."

"Okay, I'm checking the cameras…"

Himiko went silent. Erika started walking. Signs

pointed her in the direction of the statue as she waited for Himiko's response. And then it came up again.

"All right, here we go," said Himiko. "Area around the statue looks empty. Could be they're keeping their distance until they see you."

"Until they see the original courier, you mean," Erika corrected.

"Well yeah, that. You got a plan?"

"Check the surrounding area, see if there's anyone who looks suspicious," said Erika.

"What do you expect, someone in a trench coat, fedora, and sunglasses?"

"Humor me."

She could hear Himiko's sigh and then silence. There were spots of raised grass and trees scattered around the concrete. Erika sat on one of the edgings and sipped her coffee. There was a staircase just ahead and up those steps was the statue. The phone buzzed in her pocket and Erika was quick to pull it out.

"I don't see you."

Erika glanced at the surrounding area, trying to find anyone who might be using a phone. There were few people around and those who were present weren't holding any devices.

"That makes two of us," Erika typed in response.

She waited for a reply, but it didn't seem to be coming. Erika sighed and took another sip of her coffee. It didn't take long before the cup was empty. When she reached the garbage bin to throw it away, she heard a voice in her ear.

"Hey, there's someone at the statue," said Himiko.

"What do they look like?" asked Erika.

"Well…believe it or not…but it's a dude in a trench coat and fedora."

"You've got to be joking," said Erika.

"Nope. Want me to stream the footage to you."

"No, that's okay. I'm going to get closer."

Erika dropped the empty cup in the bin and started moving slowly up the steps. The green statue of Saigo Takamori started to peak over the horizon. And when she reached the summit, she saw the man Himiko had told her about.

His back was to her and he stared up at the statue. His hands were in his coat pockets and he pulled them out. Erika caught a glimpse of a device in one of his hands and he looked down. A moment later, her phone buzzed.

"No cameras. No calls."

"I see you both just standing there, looking at your phones," said Himiko.

"He knows you're listening," said Erika.

"So what now?"

Erika wasn't sure how to respond. She could make a scene and arrest him right here and now. But she had no idea who he really was and that just might make things more difficult. Especially if it was Gardner.

The phone buzzed again and her predicament was solved for her.

"I'd like to speak to you in private, Agent Kuroki."

Erika's eyes widened. He knew who she was, which meant it *had* to be Gardner. That was fine, maybe this would work out better for her. She'd confront him with the knowledge that he'd committed a crime by hiring those two bosozoku to come after her. Under that pretext, she could bring him in quietly, and he wouldn't be able to withstand interrogation.

"Drop the surveillance."

"Huh?"

"You heard me, cut the cameras. I'll call you back later."

Erika ended the call and switched her implants so any other calls that came through would be ignored. She moved slowly towards the man in the coat and he stared up at the statue. Before she came up by his side, but when she was within earshot, he started speaking.

"Right where you are is fine, Agent Kuroki."

Erika was a bit surprised, but she stopped, keeping that small distance between them.

"Do you know the story of Saigo Takamori?" he asked.

"He was a samurai, right?" she asked.

The man nodded. "That's right. He was an essential figure in the Meiji Restoration, which was the first step in Japan's modernization back in the late 1800s. Reluctantly, he was then persuaded to lead the Satsuma Rebellion against the new country he'd helped create."

"Why the history lesson?" asked Erika.

"There's an old saying that the only thing we learn from history is that we *don't* learn from history. I've always believed that history can give us a kind of roadmap, a way to avoid the mistakes of our ancestors."

"It's a nice theory, but I think it sounds a bit too simplistic."

"Maybe it is," he said. "Regardless, I've always thought about Saigo's story. He came to regret his part in what he had created and so, he sought to make amends for it."

"What happened to him?" asked Erika.

"He was injured in the battle of Shiroyama. From there,

the accounts differ. Some say he committed *seppuku*. Other scholars suggest his wounds could have driven him into shock and that his men severed his head, assisting him in the warrior's death he would have desired," he said. "One thing we can be sure of is that his revolt against what he had created led to his death. So that begs the question—was it worth it in the end?

He looked back at her. Erika was surprised when she saw his face for the first time.

"You're not Gardner Takasu..." she muttered.

He offered her a smile. He was a good deal older than Gardner—his visible hair was pure white and wrinkles lined his face. The eyes behind the round glasses he wore were warm and kind, a far cry from Gardner's steel expression.

"It can't be..." muttered Erika. But she knew she had seen that face before. The photos from the background information on this case. And the framed pictures in the apartment.

He turned to face her and then bowed. "My name is Dr. Kenjiro Miyata. I believe you've been looking for me."

CHAPTER 19

The possibility of Miyata being the one who hired the bosozoku had entered Erika's mind. After all, how could it not? But one thing she never would have expected was for Miyata himself to turn up at the hand-off. She was still somewhat at a loss for words after he introduced himself, leaving him to pick up the conversation.

"Shall we go for a walk?" he asked.

Erika opened her mouth but said nothing. She then simply gave a silent nod. Miyata gestured for her to head back for the stairs she had just come up and began walking towards the steps. Erika moved beside him.

"You know who I am," she said, still somewhat in surprise. "Am I right to assume you also know we've been looking for you?"

"I am," said Miyata.

"So if you know there's a search for you, why would you come to such a public place with cameras everywhere?"

"We can talk about that later. But what I'm more interested in is discussing some of your actions," said Miyata. "I notice, for example, that you've come alone."

"How do you know I don't have back-up?" asked Erika.

"How's that armor working out for you?" asked Miyata. "Integrates well with your implants? Response time good? Well-protected?"

"You developed the armor when you were working for Yoshida?" asked Erika.

Miyata nodded as they reached the foot of the stairs. They continued forward, approaching Chuo-dori. Miyata turned left and Erika stayed by his side.

"I developed a lot of the systems that the Tokkei use, so I was able to build a backdoor into their systems. One they haven't found yet. That's how I knew they were searching for me and how I knew that you in particular were assigned to the case," said Miyata. "I also know that my computer wasn't logged into evidence, which means they don't know you have it."

"Maybe that was done on purpose so you'd reach out. Set a trap for you," said Erika.

"Maybe. But I've known Hiro since he was in diapers. And he's a stickler for procedure. So I doubt he'd sign off on something like that. Which means you'd *have* to keep it secret."

They waited at the light until it changed, and then crossed. Erika wasn't sure if Miyata had a destination in mind or if he was just wandering.

"You know you have to come in with me," said Erika. "I've got questions to ask you about—"

Miyata nodded. "About Kitano. Yes, I'm aware. But I'm not in the mood to be tossed in a hole for something I haven't done."

"Don't be paranoid, old man. Nobody's going to throw you in any hole."

Miyata scoffed. "I take it there's a lot you don't know about law enforcement in this country. The Act on the Protection of Specially Designated Secrets grants the government broad powers in areas related to defense intelligence. And due to Yoshida's close relationship with the Defense Ministry, this crime they're trying to frame me for would definitely constitute a violation."

"Wait, frame? Who's framing you? And why?"

Miyata stopped at the next corner and turned to face Erika. "That's what I want to talk to you about. But free from the Ministry's prying eyes and ears. Which is why I'd like you to come with me."

A taxi pulled up to the curb and the rear door opened. Miyata began to climb inside, but Erika grabbed his arm. He looked back at her and she shook her head.

"I can't let you leave."

"Like I said, I want you to come with me," said Miyata. "There's a lot we have to discuss. And when I'm finished, if you don't like what I have to say, then I'll allow you to take me in to your superiors."

Erika sighed. She didn't like the idea of trusting Miyata like this without any sort of back-up whatsoever. But at the same time, she was also afraid to let him out of her sight. This might be the best way to get some information. So she climbed into the car with him.

"Fine," she said. "But this had better be good."

The door closed behind her and the AI taxi began moving down the street. Her AR-HUD flashed a notification of a missed call from a blocked number. She assumed that had to be Himiko, but she just ignored it.

"So are you going to tell me what this is all about?" she asked.

"Kitano's people were using Yoshida Tech, weren't they?"

Erika stared at Miyata. "The fact that you have that information suggests you're the reason why."

"A few months ago, I discovered some irregularities in testing results," said Miyata. "When new implants are in development, they have to undergo animal testing. Only if those are successful do we then move on to human trials. But some of the results I saw in reports suggested that they had jumped ahead of human trials."

"What do you mean?"

"As far as the records were concerned, these were classified as animal test results. But in reality, the subjects were all humans," said Miyata.

Erika's memory flashed back to the thing she and Hiro fought beneath Kitano's compound. And then she remembered what Dr. Iwata had told her when beginning the examination of the corpse.

"If the government has no record of their genetic information, then there's no way of determining the identity. They can easily be disposed of once the tests are complete and authorities have no way of tracing it back to the perpetrators. And there's no one to miss the victims, so the police don't receive any pressure from next of kin."

She also recalled the words of Takahashi, one of Kitano's men that she had tracked down.

"Refugees. They wanted to experiment on them."

"You knew, didn't you?" asked Miyata. "Or at least you suspected."

Erika looked back at him. Kitano provided the test subjects and the testing grounds, and someone inside Yoshida provided the implants. But that still didn't absolve Miyata.

"All this does is prove you knew yourself. It doesn't mean you weren't behind it," she said. "Which is why forensics found evidence of your signature on those implants."

"You saw how I was able to get into your system. And to answer your earlier question, I've managed to avoid facial recognition through a unique implant. It generates a distortion field around my face that registers false results," said Miyata. "How have you done with my computer? Broken into it yet?"

Erika shook her head.

"Exactly. So if I'm able to cover my tracks this well, what makes you think I'd be so sloppy as to leave my signature all over technology I was smuggling on the black market?"

"That's why you said you're being framed," said Erika. "But by whom?"

"That's the question. I brought my concerns to my superiors. They assured me there would be an investigation. Shortly after that, I was told that the investigation found no irregularities and that there must have been a glitch in the system."

"But you didn't believe them," said Erika.

Miyata shook his head. "I investigated it, of course. I've got resources that no one in Yoshida is truly aware of. And I learned that the investigation was quashed—by Gardner Takasu."

"You're saying Takasu was working with Kitano?"

"For the past year, Takasu has been pushing R&D to progress faster. And we tried, but while still adhering to safety protocols. Now ask yourself why the VP of government relations would be pressuring R&D."

"Because of the client," said Erika. "You're saying the Defense Ministry wanted this accelerated."

He nodded. "They've been demanding upgrades and new equipment at an increased rate over the past few years and Yoshida's been trying to meet the demand."

"So Gardner farms out the testing to Kitano, who finds subjects among the refugees he smuggles into the country."

"That's correct."

"What's on your computer? Why so much security?" asked Erika. "If it's evidence that backs this all up, why not just send it to the press or something?"

"The press won't do anything. The vagueness of the State Secrecy Law would lead to them getting a visit from the Tokkei if they tried to broadcast a single word of this." Miyata took off his glasses and rubbed his eyes. "The computer has information on my family."

"Your family…? But the records…" Erika stopped herself as she remembered the phtoographs. "Keiko Izumi? The girls?"

Miyata nodded, staring out the window. "They were orphans. We took them in, gave them a home."

"Why is there no record of any adoption?"

"Before a child can be adopted, they need legal status. These girls didn't have that. If we tried to make their adoptions official, they would have been arrested for violating immigration laws."

"What happened to them?" asked Erika.

"They're with their mother."

"Their mother…? Then Keiko Izumi…"

"Her suicide was faked," said Miyata. "We used connections I'd made through the years in order to craft new identities for both her and the girls. In another year, I was going to join them."

"And Yoshida knows about this?" asked Erika.

"Shortly after they went into hiding, I discovered a private investigator was looking into my affairs. I don't know how much he told Yoshida, but I'm sure if they could find any evidence of Keiko and the children, they'd use it against me," said Miyata. "That computer is the only thing I have to connect me to them."

"You're taking a risk by trusting me with all this information," said Erika. "Why? For what possible reason would you think you could tell me all of this?"

"Because I investigated you and your background," said Miyata. "I know you're different from most of the Tokkei."

"And how do you know that?"

"Your father, for one."

Erika closed her eyes and took a deep breath. "You knew my father?"

"No, nothing like that," said Miyata. "But I knew of him. He was a good man."

"Yeah, so good that he abandoned his wife and child to a life of struggle."

Miyata gave her a concerned look. His eyes conveyed warmth and sympathy. It was a look Erika hadn't seen in another person in longer than she could remember.

"Do you really believe that?" he asked.

"It's not a matter of belief, but fact," said Erika.

"Your father was a champion of human rights. He died protesting the government. I find it hard to believe that he'd ever abandon anyone. Especially not his own family."

"Maybe he wasn't quite the man you imagine," said Erika.

"Fair enough. But let me ask you a question—why did you enlist?"

Erika gave him an incredulous look. "You're the second person in as many days to ask me that question."

"And?"

"I needed the money," she said.

"That's what I thought. Based on your psychological evaluations, you aren't an ideologue. And I've also got some personal testimonials."

"What does that mean?" asked Erika.

Miyata rested his head on the back of his seat and closed his eyes. "You'll find out soon."

Erika sighed and looked out her own window. She didn't recognize where they were and she brought up the map on the console before her. The screen read, "CAN-NOT LOAD DATA." She looked back at Miyata.

"What's going on? Where are we?"

"There's one more thing I have to show you, Agent Kuroki," said Miyata. "You see, I've been looking for someone like you for a while. Someone I believe I can rely on."

Erika lunged for Miyata and braced her forearm against his throat. She raised her other hand in a closed fist.

"I may not be armed, but I don't need to be to kill you."

Miyata gasped, his eyes bulging in their sockets. He struggled to get the words out. "I—I believe you…"

"So tell me why I shouldn't kill you right now."

He gagged, struggling to speak. Erika weakened her grip just enough so he could speak clearly.

"If you kill me, the car will still proceed to its preprogrammed destination. You won't be able to override it, nor will you be able to escape," he said. "And once you get where you're going, I don't think my associates will be too happy with what you've done."

"Tell me what's going on."

"Just sit back and be patient," said Miyata. "You'll find out soon enough."

Erika's arms tensed. Her training told her she should snap his neck and then try and figure a way out of here. But she had an instinct that he'd been honest with her the whole time. And that was more than she could say about what she'd heard from many others lately, particularly her superiors.

"We'll do it your way for now," she said as she sat back in her seat. "But you're on thin ice."

CHAPTER 20

The taxi finally came to a stop in an underground parking garage. When the doors opened, Erika stepped out and took stock of her surroundings. There didn't seem to be any other vehicles in the garage. Erika faced Miyata, her fingers curling into fists.

"Okay, you've got your chance. Now are you going to tell me what we're doing here? What do you want with me?"

Lights came on from behind Erika. She turned and saw headlines on her. Two shadows moved in front of the lights, one larger and one much slimmer. The lights died and Erika recognized the two figures.

"Ishiyama? Himiko?"

They both moved closer. Masao folded his arms over his broad chest and Himiko stood with her hands resting on her hips. Erika was still looking between the two of them as if she were trying to determine whether or not they actually stood in front of her.

"What's going on?" she asked.

"Miyata has been leading a resistance group for some time," said Masao. "In fact, it was the whole reason I joined the Jietai in the first place, to try to work my way up the ladder and get into a position of power."

"And I'm the one who roped the big guy into this," said Himiko.

"So that's what this is all about? You've been trying to get me to sign up?" asked Erika.

"You now know what Yoshida and the Ministry are up to. You saw the results of their experiments when you went after Kitano," said Miyata. "These are gross violations of human rights and we can't do this on our own."

"I was keeping tabs on you when we were stationed together overseas. Paying attention to the way you operated, how you acted with the other soldiers and the locals," said Masao. "Most *hafu* who enlist try to overcompensate for their foreign blood. But not you. And then when you came to me about needing some help outside the Ministry, I realized we could trust you."

"And all due respect to Agent Ishiyama, I still wasn't completely convinced. Hence why I had Himiko meet with you in person," said Miyata.

"Is that why you contacted me once Himiko brought me to her place?" asked Erika.

"Yeah, I sent a quick message saying I was onboard," said Himiko.

"That was why I decided we'd meet at Ueno. Speaking with you and seeing that you indeed came alone was everything I needed to know that you are a woman of your word," said Miyata. "That's why I'm willing to trust you."

"What do you expect me to do?" asked Erika. "Rebel

against the Tokkei? Start a revolution?"

"A revolution isn't that simple and if we blow your cover, then we'd lose a valuable resource, now wouldn't we?" asked Miyata. "Trying to launch a revolt against the entire government would just result in instant defeat. They'd bring the full force of the Jietai and the Tokkei down upon us and we'd be crushed. We need a scalpel, not a shotgun."

"How do we do that?" asked Erika.

"If we released the documents we've got, that alone wouldn't be enough," said Himiko. "Most people wouldn't bother reading through all that and they wouldn't be reported on. But if we had some actual footage of what was happening and broadcast that across the internet, it'd be hard to ignore. There would *have* to be a response."

Erika glanced at Himiko. "And how do you expect to get that?"

"You were tasked with investigating Kitano's men," said Masao. "But I checked the reports and you wrote that they were a dead end. Was that true?"

"I found one of them—Takahashi—and confronted him," said Erika.

"And what did you learn?" asked Miyata.

"He told me what you did and also said there's an island where the successful subjects are taken," said Erika.

"That island's where we can get what we need. We can document on video what's been done," said Himiko. "But we haven't been able to find out where it is."

"Kuroki, did he give any indication of where that island might be?" asked Masao.

Erika sighed and nodded. "More than that. He told me the name of the island."

"Seriously?" asked Himiko. "We've been trying to

figure that out and he just *told* you straight-up?"

"Did you check it out?" asked Masao.

Erika shook her head. "I wanted to, but Hiro—Agent Yoshida confronted me about it. He said the investigation was over and that I should report that Takahashi was a dead end."

"We need to get someone on that island," said Himiko. "Get footage of what's being done to these people and broadcast the shit out of it."

"Which island is it, Agent Kuroki?" asked Miyata.

"Hachijo-kojima," said Erika.

Miyata looked to Himiko next. "Does that fit with any of your research?"

"I never found any mention of any Yoshida holdings on that island," said Himiko. "But that's not unusual. They might have it hidden away in some shell companies."

"Or maybe it's not a Yoshida holding. Could be government," said Masao. "But there's no doubt something that sensitive will be well-guarded. Getting in won't be easy."

"But *can* you do it?" asked Miyata.

Masao took a deep breath and tilted his head back in thought. "I really don't know. Even with Himiko in my ear on tech support, this is gonna be an uphill climb."

Miyata turned his gaze from Masao to Erika. Soon, both Masao and Himiko's eyes also fell on her. Erika met each of their stares, beginning to sense what they were hinting at. And in response, she shook her head.

"You can't be serious," she said. "All due respect, but as skilled as Ishiyama is, he can't break into some kind of island installation."

"Not even with you by his side?" asked Miyata.

Erika shook her head. "Not at all. Maybe if we had our

Tokkei armor, but that's not an option."

"Why not?" asked Masao.

Erika's eyes bulged as she heard his response. "Please don't tell me you've been wearing that thing on non-Tokkei business. Because they can track it. And they have the means to shut it down if need be."

Masao smiled and looked at Miyata and Himiko. They also wore smiles on their faces and then all three began to chuckle. Erika was starting to feel like she was losing her mind.

"Why are you laughing?" she asked. "Is there something I missed?"

"I developed the technology for that armor, Agent Kuroki," said Miyata. "Don't you think I'd know how to override it?"

"You're telling me you can disable the Tokkei's ability to track and control us?" she asked.

Miyata nodded. "Precisely. And I can do much more than that. All I need is for you to bring it to me and I can handle the rest."

"That's the pitch, Kuroki," said Masao. "So there's only one question left—you in or you out?"

浪人

Erika stood on the roof and looked out at the night lights of Tokyo off in the distance. She had agreed to Miyata's offer, at least in this instance. She wasn't comfortable with the idea of becoming some kind of revolutionary, but she knew that she couldn't just stand by as innocent people were being experimented on for the benefit of Yoshida Tech's bottom line.

Her reflexes were as on-point as ever and as soon as

she sensed a presence, Erika immediately turned and went on the defensive, readying a fighting stance. Masao stood behind her and offered his hands up in surrender.

"Sorry, didn't mean to sneak up on you like that," he said.

Erika relaxed and looked back at the city. She still felt strange whenever she looked at Masao. First their drunken night together and now finding out that he was actually a spy working against the Tokkei.

"Are they done yet?" she asked.

"Not yet. Reprogramming the nanosuits can take some time."

After she agreed to help, Erika returned home to retrieve her armor, then brought it back so Miyata and Himiko could work on it. She was growing impatient waiting for them to finish.

Masao moved closer to her, but he still kept some distance between them. "While they're doing their thing, I thought we might have a chance to talk. I know this might all seem pretty overwhelming to you right now."

"That's putting it mildly…" she muttered. "Why did you do it anyway?"

"Join up with Miyata and Himiko?" he asked.

She nodded.

"I told you, I grew up in a rough neighborhood. Lots of workers from abroad, coming here to take up low-paying jobs in fields like construction. I grew up with people like that, so I never had the kind of 'us vs them' mentality you see in so many others, especially in the Tokkei."

"What was the trigger?" asked Erika. "Something had to have happened to make you go from hard-luck case to rebel."

"You remember James from the bar?" asked Masao. "Well, he had an older brother, Andy. The two of them, Himiko and me, we were inseperable as kids. But as we got older, Andy fell in with a different crowd. Found his way into a bosozoku gang, dropped out of school, then eventually started doing some low-level enforcer work for one of the yakuza outfits. And then he was killed in a Tokkei sting operation."

"And you blame the government for that?" asked Erika, giving him a disgusted look. "I'm sorry about your friend, but—"

"But what?" asked Masao, meeting her gaze with a harsh intensity. "But he was a criminal? But he dug his own grave? You think I haven't heard all that before?"

Masao sighed and looked down.

"It's easy for most people to just dismiss this kind of stuff. But what other choices did Andy have? Their dad died in a construction accident and the company refused to pay any benefits because he was a contract worker. His mom had trouble finding work that paid well and they were denied public assistance. Not many jobs for people like them, so Andy fell in with the bosozoku as a way to make money."

Erika's head felt heavy after hearing Masao finish the story. She thought of the struggles her own mother had in trying to make ends meet. Remembered waking up at night sometimes to hear her mother softly crying in the next room. She still didn't completely agree with Masao, but his story was enough to make her feel guilty about her earlier dismissal of it.

"I...I don't know what to say."

Masao took a deep breath. "You don't have to say

anything. But that made me realize that there's something rotten in this society. Desperation makes even the best people turn to extreme actions. And I felt like there was something I could do. Himiko was already involved with some anti-government work, so she put me in touch with some of them. They told me that what they needed was someone on the inside and they hadn't had any luck trying to turn existing agents. So I joined the Jietai in hopes of working my way up the ranks and eventually getting into the Tokkei."

"And now you've brought me into the fold, too."

"Have I?" he asked.

Erika looked him in the eyes, but then she quickly broke contact. "I don't know about all of that. I think you're doing the right thing in this instance…trying to help those people. But beyond that…"

"You still don't really realize what it is we're up against," said Masao.

"There is something broken, you're right about that. I just don't know if burning down the whole system is the way to change it," said Erika. "Can you understand where I'm coming from?"

Masao nodded. "Sure, I can understand it. Because I used to be that way, too. I felt that maybe within the Jietai, I could work to change things. But in the war, my view changed. And since being promoted to the Tokkei, I've come to realize that maybe more drastic action is necessary."

Erika turned and looked at him. "Listen, I want to help you this time. But after we're done, I think it's best if we go our separate ways. I don't want to get you in trouble, but I also don't want to lie for you."

"What are you saying?" he asked.

"I'm saying that once we finish this job, I'm going to put in for a transfer to another Tokkei branch," said Erika. "I don't want to get in the way of your work, but I also just can't get involved in this. And I'm afraid that if I stay, that's what will happen."

Masao's eyes drifted a little and his eyelids started to fall. His lips tightened slightly and he had what Erika could have sworn was a sad look on his face. But it was gone almost as soon as it had appeared.

"I get it," he said. "This kind of life ain't for everyone. And I appreciate you willing to do that for me."

"Thanks for understanding," she said.

"Yeah, no problem." He paused and silence filled the void for a few moments. Then, he added in a much lighter tone, "Besides, if you *did* turn me in, I'd just name you as my accomplice anyway."

Erika scoffed. "And here I thought you were a gentleman."

Masao let out a loud laugh in response. Erika found his laughter infectious and joined in herself. It only lasted for a short while and when their laughter had subsided, the silence had returned.

CHAPTER 21

Hachijo-kojima was a small island in the Izu archipelago, located off the coast of the larger Hachijo. Its length was just under two miles with a width measuring less than a mile. During the Edo era, both Hachijo islands were used as a place of exile for criminals. Hachijo-kojima was surrounded by high cliffs and the strait separating it from Hachijo had a powerfully strong current, making swimming or rafting all but impossible. For these reasons, the most serious criminals were exiled to the smaller island.

It had been uninhabited since 1969, but it had remained a popular destination for fishermen, divers, and explorers. At least until several years earlier, when it had been purchased from the government through Yoshida shell companies and declared private property.

Erika looked out the window in the rear of the small prop plane. Miyata had arranged for a smuggler to transport them close enough to the island and from there, they were on their own. They flew low the whole way to remain under radar. And she could see the peak of Mt. Taihei, which was the tallest point on the island breaking over the horizon. She took a deep breath and looked at Masao, who seemed utterly calm and at ease.

"Are you ready for this?" she asked.

Masao gave her a look of surprise. "Am *I* ready? Shouldn't I be asking *you* that?"

"Maybe. Just nervous about whether or not Miyata's as good as he claims. Because if it turns out that he couldn't prevent the Tokkei from tracking us, then…"

Masao grinned. "Give it a try."

Erika took a deep breath and tapped the nanite container. She closed her eyes as she felt them flow across her body and once the armor was deployed, she opened them again. When she looked down at herself, she was surprised to see that the configuration had changed.

"It's red?" she asked.

"Just a slight change, but enough to signal that we're not Tokkei," said Masao. "The rest of the armor's capabilities should be working just fine."

*"Well, **almost** fine."*

Erika heard a voice through the implants in her ears and an image of Himiko appeared on her AR-HUD.

"What does that mean?" asked Erika.

"You're cut off from the Tokkei database, so you won't be able to access any of their records," said Himiko. *"Giving you access to their systems might mean they could backtrace. Regardless of how well the data is encrypted, best not to take the risk."*

"So what if we need some intel?" asked Erika.

"That's what I'm here for. I'm your contact point with the outside world."

"You ever do anything like this before?" Erika asked Masao.

"Up until this point, it's mostly been passing intel. This is the first time I'm going into a combat situation on behalf of the group."

"So we're both new to this." In some ways, that idea was comforting to her. At least her and Masao were on the same page. On the other hand, she felt some trepidation going in without anyone who had experience in this sort of operation. Was there even any guarantee that the armor was invulnerable to Tokkei manipulation?

"We're getting close to the drop!" the pilot called from the front of the plane.

Masao activated his armor as well and went to the rear door. He pulled it open and they looked at the dark water whipping below. They didn't have time to wait. Masao looked at Erika and gestured to the open door.

"Ladies first," he said.

"Aren't you the gentlemen…"

Erika took position at the open door. She looked at Masao and he nodded. After returning the nod, Erika dove from the plane, head-first. The AR-HUD displayed the distance from the water, closing in fast, and she broke through the surface.

She looked around the underwater landscape, her nightvision activating to allow her to see clearly in the darkness. A moment later, Masao crashed through the surface.

"How are we on comms?" he asked. "You hear me?"

"You're coming in loud and clear," she replied. "And me?"

Masao gave a thumbs-up.

Their armor was water-tight and had a limited supply of oxygen. It was enough for them to approach the island unseen and begin their infiltration of the compound. Their HUDs displayed a topographical map of the area, indicating their presence in the ocean and their destination. The northwestern coast offered the easiest point of entry onto the island, and that's where they were headed.

They reached the rocky shore without problem and emerged from the water. The rocks sloped up into a tree-dotted mountainside leading all the way up to the summit. But the scans were returning no signs.

"This can't be right…" she muttered.

"What's wrong?" asked Masao.

"The scanners aren't picking up anything. No life signs, no energy signatures, nothing."

"You're sure it wasn't the larger Hachijo?"

"Positive, wouldn't forget something like that," said Erika.

"Maybe the guy was wrong," he said, then changed tactics. "Himiko, any ideas?"

"We can't get any sense of what's happening on the island. Been trying to get a better view with satellites, but we haven't seen a damn thing. For all intents and purposes, this place looks abandoned."

"This can't just be a total bust," said Erika. "We didn't come all the way here for nothing."

"We gotta check the island. First, let's try and get a better picture of it."

Masao's *kabuto*—or the outer portion of the helmet—detached itself from his head and reconfigured itself into a small drone. Without the *kabuto*, all he was left with was the *mengu* armor that covered his face and stretched all around his head.

The drone-helmet flew away from them, fading into the darkness as it began to approach the mountain. Erika wasn't aware that the armor had a built-in drone, but then there were still a lot of things she didn't know about this suit. Later, she would have to ask Miyata to give her a full tutorial of all its systems.

She caught herself on that. *Later?* This was supposed to be a one-time thing. Once her and Masao captured the necessary footage proving what Yoshida was up to at this facility, that would be it. She'd leave Miyata and the rest of his rebellion behind, put in for a transfer, and then once she completed her term of duty, she'd retire from the government and go into the private sector.

"Anything interesting?" she asked Masao after several moments of silence.

Masao shook his head. "Nothing yet. I don't get it. We know Yoshida owns this island through shell companies, we know it's been shut down from any visitation, but I'm not seeing anything here. Not even a port." He cast his gaze in Erika's direction. "Didn't Takahashi tell you that they brought them here by boat?"

"Yeah, he did," said Erika.

"So if they're bringing people in by boat, where do they dock? You figure it'd have to be a decent-sized craft, but there's no infrastructure for that. And it doesn't seem likely that they anchor offshore and then bring people in by raft."

"No, you're right..." Erika looked down at the dark water. Nothing showed up on Himiko's satellite imagery and Masao's drone couldn't turn up anything of note, either. There *had* to be something else.

A thought occurred to her. Erika went to the edge of the rocky shore and dove back into the water. She started circling the island, relying on her armor's sensors to make sure she didn't lose her place.

"What are you doing?" asked Masao over their comms.

"What if it's not a boat?" asked Erika.

"What?"

"No dock, nothing visible on the surface, and this is an extinct volcano," said Erika. "What if everything is hidden under the surface?"

"Hey, Kuroki, I'm glad you're thinkin' outside the box," came Himiko's voice, *"but try not to go off the reservation here, okay?"*

"What other option is there?" asked Erika. "There's *something* here, I'm sure of it."

"Oh god, I feel like I'm taking crazy pills…" muttered Himiko.

"Erika, you're sure about this?" asked Masao.

"Not sure, but I have to check it out."

Masao said nothing for a few moments and then he responded with, *"Okay, but don't take too much time. The suit's got a limited oxygen supply."*

Erika was aware of that as she swam through the water. She continued going lower, then circled around the length of the island. Soon, she would have to emerge to replenish her oxygen supply. And she was worried about possibly being spotted by something.

But then, her armor alerted her to something behind her. Erika retreated, finding a cove to conceal herself. She could see lights off in the distance, moving across the landscape. She focused her sights and zoomed in on the craft.

"Himiko, are you seeing this?" she whispered.

*"Is…is that…a **submarine**?"*

"Just what I suspected," said Erika. "It's not what's on the surface that matters, but what's underneath. They've been ferrying these people via sub into a complex hidden inside the remnants of the volcano."

CHAPTER 22

Erika moved closer towards the oncoming sub as it traversed the ocean floor. She was careful to avoid falling into the path of its lights. But being detected wasn't the only thing she had to worry about. An alert began flashing on her AR-HUD, warning that her armor's limited oxygen supply was at risk of depletion.

"Kuroki, you've got to surface. That suit's not equipped to stay submerged for that long," said Himiko over the comms.

"Then stop talking to me so I don't have to waste oxygen to respond," said Erika.

On her AR-HUD, she could see Himiko's exasperated frown. She understood why the hacker was worried about her, but she was also worried that if there was some hidden entrance, this might be her only chance to get inside the compound.

Fortunately, there were larger creatures beneath the ocean than her. She was unlikely to be picked up by the submarine's radar. And even if it did, her presence would likely be dismissed as just a big fish. But she had to make sure she got inside.

As the submarine passed, Erika followed it, moving into its wake. The alert continued to flash, warning that now, only 15% of her oxygen supply remained.

The sub's wake made it difficult to press forward. Its propulsion made her kick twice as hard to advance the same distance. With the increased physical activity, her muscles demanded more oxygen to keep up. And that just depleted her supply even further.

The display now read 12%. The vertical bar that represented her oxygen supply was low and red, continuing to flash warnings at her. She could see the image Himiko's frightened expression in the upper righthand corner of her AR-HUD.

Erika tried to ignore both of them. If she allowed herself to lose her cool, if she fell into fear's grip, there would be no escape. Her body would quickly use up what remained of the oxygen supply.

There was only one choice left. It was one she had been against because it could draw unwanted attention from the submarine's sensors. But that had now become a risk she had to take if she was going to survive.

Erika activated the thrusters on her suit, pushing her forward through the water. She streaked directly for the sub, leaving her own wake. The thrusters were good for boosts on land and in sea, but they were meant for short, quick bursts to gain an advantage. Like the suit's oxygen, they weren't built for sustained use and the power levels were dropping. But all she needed was to get within reach…
Erika extended her arm, her fingers stretching as far as they could to try and find purchase…

And then…

Success!

Her fingers touched the side of the sub and the nanites adhered to its surface. Erika pulled her free hand towards the sub and set it in place, so now the nanites had cemented both hands to its surface.

7% oxygen left. Erika closed her eyes and controlled her breathing. Slow, deep breaths. She had to lower her heart rate and keep her breathing in check. Each breath had to be an essential one. And she had to just hope that they reached the complex before her oxygen ran out.

It was now down to 4%. The oxygen had grown thin and with each passing moment, that only got worse. A feeling of lightheadedness started to overtake her, but she wouldn't allow herself to panic.

2% left. This was it. She was on her last legs.

Erika took a deep breath and held it in, the last breath the suit was capable of providing. She had never really been a believer in the Shinto gods, but now she found herself praying for their deliverance.

The sub's forward movement halted. Erika opened her eyes and looked to the craft's rear. A pair of mechanized doors were now sliding shut behind them. And the sub began to rise. She could see the surface of the water, but if she emerged too quickly, there was risk of discovery.

Gotta chance it… she thought as she activated her thrusters to push her through the surface. Erika's head burst through the water and her suit responded automatically to the presence of oxygen, allowing air into the armor. Erika breathed deeply and saw the oxygen bar slowly refilling.

Her sensors began picking up movement. She had to get out of the water. Erika raised her arm and a piton attached to a cable fired from her gauntlet. It found purchase in the ceiling above and once it was secure, Erika retracted the cable and she rapidly ascended up into the darkness overhead. She found a spot right above the docked sub, crouching low to perch on one of the rafters, her curved back almost pressed against the ceiling.

The submarine now rested in a pool of water. A gangway extended from a space breaking the guardrails as a group of people emerged from an adjoining doorway, moving towards the sub. The gangway made contact and a door opened on the sub. All the people in the room wore non-descript work uniforms with balaclavas hiding their faces.

"Himiko, are you getting this?"

"Yeah, I see 'em," said Himiko. "Stay hidden."

A man emerged from the sub, moving down the gang-way and onto solid ground. He nodded to people that met him upon disembarkation, then turned to face the sub. There were shouts in English of "Go! Go!"

One by one, people emerged from the ship. Erika activated the visual receptors' binocular vision and they zoomed in on the people. They were older or in an infirm state.

"It's just as Takahashi said…" she muttered in a low whisper. "He told me they kept a few for their own experiments, but that most were brought here. Older people, those with disabilities…it's all true…"

"I know it's hard," Himiko's voice had lost some of its edge, *"but this isn't enough. We need footage of what's going on here."*

Erika swallowed her emotions and gave a nod. "You're right. Masao, what's your location?"

"I've been scouting the area trying to find another way in, but haven't found anything yet."

"Can you come in the same way I did?" she asked.

"Probably not," said Himiko. "You got lucky with that sub. But I watched the footage from your suit and I saw those doors looked pretty thick. Even if Masao's sword could cut through it, he'd run out of oxygen first."

"I can't leave her alone in there," said Masao.

"I agree and I'm not saying you should," said Himiko. "But I've got an idea."

"What do you suggest?" asked Erika.

"Place like this has to have some sort of security control center. If you can find it, then not only could you give Masao a way in, but you can also disable any systems that might get in your way and download a map of the compound," said Himiko. "Basically, it'd make everything go a lot smoother."

"Right, if I can find it," said Erika. "Masao, just sit tight and stay hidden. Even though we didn't see anything on the surface, that doesn't mean there isn't the possibility of some kind of patrol."

"Gotcha. Don't leave me waiting **too** long, Kuroki. I get antsy."

"Kuroki, look around the room. Slowly," said Himiko. "I need to see if there's some way out of there. Other than the public exit."

"What about these people?" asked Erika.

"Much as it sucks to say, you can't help them right now. You show yourself, the place goes on lockdown and sends all their security after you. And we have no idea just how powerful that security would be."

Erika sighed. She felt somewhat ineffective, but she knew Himiko was right. Slowly, Erika turned her head, trying to notice every single nook and cranny, finding some potential exit.

"Wait, go back," said Himiko. *"Look down just a bit and to your left."*

Erika did as she was told. In the corner of her AR-HUD, Himiko's face was replaced by a replay of what she had recorded from Erika's suit. A small part was highlighted by Himiko. Erika looked in realtime and zoomed in.

"It's a vent," said Himiko.

"Can I even *fit* in there?"

"Only one way to find out. But you gotta do it quietly. Don't know how long it will take for them to empty that sub and we don't want to waste time."

She was right. The rafters were a bit too close to the ceiling to easily move around, so Erika would have to cross by jumping. She dropped from the rafter and grabbed it. Erika swung a few times before releasing her grip. She moved across the distance and grabbed the next rafter, pausing for a moment and waiting to see if there was any recognition from below.

None of them looked up.

Erika took a breath, then swung, released, and flew to the next rafter. Now that she was beginning to get the hang of it, she moved with more freedom. Still, she didn't let herself get cocky, trying to maintain some degree of patience. Moving too fast might generate enough noise to draw unwanted attention. But if she was too slow, then every moment she stayed in one place would also increase the risk of discovery. Maintaining a balance between the two was most important.

Voices rose up from below. Erika froze and pulled herself up to the rafters. She squeezed between the beam and the ceiling, staring down with bated breath. One of the prisoners had stumbled and fallen while disembarking and now they were shouting at him. He was an old man, probably well into his eighties or nineties, and clearly had difficulty moving. But that didn't stop the masked enforcers from violently pulling him to his feet and shouting insults in a mixture of English and Japanese.

Erika's muscles tensed. She could feel the urge to draw her sword and cut through each of those masked monsters. The nanites started to form the hilt in her hand and all it took was a simple thought to activate the energy blade.

"Kuroki, why are your weapons systems coming online?" asked Himiko.

"I can't just let this happen…"

"Stop it, you're no good to anyone if you're dead!"

"They wouldn't even be able to touch me."

"Erika, listen to her," said Masao. *"Maybe **they** can't hurt you, but remember what you and Hiro faced in Yoshiwara? We don't know **what** they've got locked away."*

She froze in place, muscles still tensed and ready to explode. But she stayed calm and relaxed her hand, the nanites that formed the hilt retreating to her armor. Silently, Erika apologized to the old man, trying to look away as the sounds of their blunt weapons striking him and his cries of pain echoed in the docking area.

They were distracted now and as much as she hated to think like this, it gave her a chance to quickly close the gap between her and the only possible escape route. Erika dropped down and grabbed the rafter, then resumed swinging from beam to beam.

She crossed the distance quickly and now she saw the vent. It was covered by a grating and that would provide difficulty. Erika perched on the beam and this time, she did activate her sword. She swung it for the vent, but it fell just short of hitting the grate.

"Dammit…" she muttered. "Gotta try something else."

She moved across the beam until she reached the wall. When she placed her hands on the wall's surface, the nanites adhered. She brougth her other hand to the wall and moved over its surface. Going slow was even more important. Now she no longer had the benefit of the shadows above. If any of those guards looked in her direction, they would easily spot her.

Erika's heart started to pound in her chest as she crawled across. She paused every few seconds and looked back to the ground to see if any guards were at risk of spotting her. Once she was confident she was safe, she continued to the corner and the vent that represented her freedom.

The hilt formed in her hand, but she changed the setting on the blade to shorten it. Now it was the equivalent of a *wakizashi* or short sword. Erika raised the blade above her head and began cutting into the grate. Sparks flew and she moved slowly so as not to make too much noise. Erika looked below frequently to ensure that no one was looking up. And though she hated to think about it, the guards' belligerent nature towards the prisoners actually helped cover up the sounds of her cutting.

The grate gave way and she pulled it free from its mount. Erika wrapped her arm around the grate and crawled up. The attachments on her armor wouldn't enable her to enter, so as Erika pulled herself into the vent, the nanites retreated, collapsing her suit. She was less protected that way, but it meant she could move with more freedom.

At least she had made it through the first part. Now she just had to find the control center.

CHAPTER 23

The ventilation shaft proved to be a tight fit for Erika, even without her armor. It was slow-going, using her forearms to move inch by inch through the shaft. Whenever she came to a vent opening, she stopped to look through the grating to see where she was.

Without the armor, she wasn't able to use her scanners to try and get a better idea of where the control room was. Time was a factor, so she couldn't spend too long trying to find the center.

The lack of the armor also meant she had no connection to Himiko or Masao. Her regular cellular implants weren't equipped with the kind of encryption needed for secure communication, at least not as advanced as her armor.

The shaft was bathed in darkness and she didn't have her armor's nightvision. Whenever there was an opening, some light filtered through, but not enough to truly navigate. She mostly had to move by touch.

She felt the shaft inclining upwards, which just made

it more difficult to move. Erika focused her thoughts on that old man she saw getting beat up by the guards. She thought about the poor test subject she had to kill back in Yoshiwara. And then she remembered how all of this was being done by Yoshida to provide the Ministry of Defense with the kind of weaponry they demanded. Those thoughts provided fuel for her to push forward and at a greater pace, despite the narrow fit and fighting against gravity.

Erika reached her hand forward and felt cold metal. She looked left, then right, and saw some light filtering through a grate towards the right. She had reached a junction and she had to bend and twist her body in order to turn to the right. It was a struggle, but those thoughts continued to urge her forward.

After some doing, she had completed the turn and continued her trek. The grate was just ahead and as with the others, she slowed as she peered through the bars.

She was over a large room and there were several people inside. All were dressed in the same nondescript uniforms with balaclava masks. Erika counted a total of four. There were holographic monitors and the men sat at terminals. She couldn't quite make out what was on the monitors from this angle, but this seemed likely to be the control center she was looking for.

Erika grabbed the grating and pushed. It was fixed in tightly, but it came loose and fell to the ground below. As soon as it clattered there, the guards turned to look at the source.

Before they could truly react, Erika dropped from the opening and landed in a crouch. She activated the container and the nanites spread across her body, reforming her armor.

The guard furthest from her drew his sidearm and opened fire. The bullets were unable to penetrate the armor and just ricocheted off. One of the ricochets hit the guard closest to her as he was about to fire his own weapon.

Erika lunged for the guard firing. She grabbed the barrel of his gun and pulled it from his grip, then delivered a powerful kick to his sternum. He jolted back, slamming into the wall and causing the holographic monitors to flicker.

A third guard tried to strike from behind with a baton. It broke against Erika's *mento*. She turned and he tried to attack with what remained of the baton. Erika grabbed his arm and twisted, breaking his wrist. Her free hand curled into a fist, and she slammed it into the side of his face, knocking him unconscious. She released his wrist and he slumped to the ground.

Only one guard remained. Erika faced him and he held his gun. Saying he had it aimed at her would be generous—his body shook so drastically with fear that he was more likely to shoot the ground than her. Erika closed the distance just a little with a single step. The guard immediately jumped back, hitting the rolling chair behind him. He stumbled over it, nearly falling, and tried to push the chair at Erika.

She grabbed it with one hand and easily swung it to the wall. Erika grabbed the gun just as he squeezed the trigger, firing a round into her palm. Erika tore the gun away and quickly disassembled it.

"I-I just work here…" he muttered in a pathetic plea.

In response, Erika grabbed his head and brought it down, striking it with her raised knee.

"Himiko, I'm in the control center."

"Took you long enough."

"Give me a break, I had to crawl through a tight tunnel and then fight off some guards." On Erika's AR-HUD, the armor informed her that it couldn't find a wireless signal. "I think everything here is hardwired. I'm not finding any signals."

"Check the equipment. You should be able to plug in somewhere."

Doing as Himiko suggested, Erika looked around the room and examined the equipment. There was a cabinet with several different devices. She checked each one until she found a port. Erika raised her finger and the nanites rose above the tip, forming into a connector that she slid into the port. Her AR-HUD opened up a new window, showing what it was getting from the server.

"I'm downloading surveillance footage from the past six months, should give you exactly what you need," said Erika.

"Does that mean we're done?" asked Masao. *"You don't need my help after all?"*

As she tapped into the surveillance records, Erika was also able to view the live footage. She found cameras located in a detention area where a number of old and infirm refugees were locked up, with far more people than should be held in a single cell.

"We're not done," said Erika. "We have to help these people."

"That's not why you're there," said Himiko.

"I'm not leaving them like this. It's inhumane," said Erika.

"How are you gonna get them outta there?"

"The sub. Get them onboard and take them back to the mainland."

"And then what? They're non-entities without legal status. They'll be rounded up and sent right back here or somewhere else. That's assuming they aren't killed outright."

It would be easy to simply accuse Himiko of being cold, but she was also right. Without anywhere to take these people, would getting them out of here just be giving them false hope? Erika knew she wouldn't be able to look at herself in the mirror tomorrow morning if she just walked away.

"I can't do it," said Erika. "I know we're in a tough spot, but I can't continue turning a blind eye to these people."

Himiko didn't have a response. Erika waited, staring at her uncertain face in the AR-HUD. Then Masao's face took priority.

"Tell me how to get inside, I'm gonna help you."

"Wait, you're going in?" asked Himiko with surprise. *"Guys, listen. I **know** this sucks. But if you're caught, you'll be tortured and they **will** eventually break you."*

"Maybe, but she's right. We can't just leave these people behind. It's worth the risk," said Masao.

"Okay, I'm looking for layouts of the installation," said Erika. She downloaded the maps and transmitted them to Masao and Himiko. "There's a maintenance hatch on the south side of the island. I've marked it on the map. Once you're inside, get to the sub and get it ready to depart."

"That it?"

"For now, yeah. Stay in touch," said Erika.

浪人

Masao entered the facility through the maintenance hatch Erika told him about. He jumped down into a small alcove without bothering to use the provided ladder. His sensors told him there were no lifeforms detected, but he still pressed up against the narrow wall as he peered around the alcove's corner to confirm.

The map provided by Erika was superimposed in a corner of his AR-HUD, with a blinking light displaying his current location and another showing the submarine bay that was his destination.

"You read me, Masao?"

It was Himiko, her face appearing on his AR-HUD. "Yeah, what's up?"

"We're on a private channel because I wanted to talk about Kuroki."

"She's coming through pretty well, huh? Was I right about her or what?"

Silence lingered in his ear as he moved silently down the corridor. Erika may have been capable of squeezing through the air ducts, but he knew he couldn't do the same. He had to focus on the armor's scanners and stealth.

"Himiko? You still there?"

"We've got a difference of opinion, big guy. She's risking this whole operation just to save a few lives."

"Thought that's what we were trying to do."

"Think big picture. If you guys are captured, they can find out about Miyata and me. And if we go down, everything we've been working towards is over. We've got to have some priorities here."

"So what do you propose? We get out of here right now? Leave those people to whatever grim fate's waiting for them?"

In the midst of another pause, Masao entered a stairwell heading down. He could have sworn he heard Himiko sigh. He'd known her long enough to know that she wasn't as hard or as cold as she pretended. Even contemplating what she'd been saying would end up haunting her. All the more reason why he had to stand firm against her.

"It's not ideal…"

"There's an understatement." He began his descent down the staircase. "Besides, you heard her, she's got her mind set on this. She's not going to just walk away."

"Yeah, I've been thinking about that…"

Masao felt his blood turn cold. "Why do I get the feeling I'm not going to like what you're about to say?"

Another pause, another sigh. And then, *"We've got the data we need. What if…what if you get out on your own?"*

He froze. Not only because he came to the bottom of the stairs, but also because of what Himiko had just suggested.

"You want to leave her behind?"

"Like you said, she's stubborn. She's going to see this through to the end. But there's no reason you have to sacrifice yourself, too. Even with everything we've told her, there's still a lot about our operation that she doesn't know. Who we're working with, where our resources come from, she's in the dark on all of that."

"I can't believe I'm hearing this…"

"C'mon, man. What do you want from me? I like her, I really do. But I've got to play this smart."

"If we become the kind of people who are willing to just sacrifice others because it's convenient, then what makes us any better than the likes of the Tokkei?" asked Masao. "What makes us any better than the people who killed your husband?"

Masao opened the door to the stairwell, careful as he peered from side to side. He stepped into the corridor and followed it to the left. Just ahead was the submarine bay.

"You still there?" he asked. "Your face hasn't moved in some time."

"Watch your back in there, okay? There's no telling what kind of secrets Yoshida has locked up in this place."

Masao smiled beneath his faceplate. That was more like the Himiko he knew. She was in a tough place and the things they saw had hardened them. But he knew there was a part of her that would never get so hard that she'd willingly sacrifice her own humanity in order to accomplish her goals.

The doors opened and he entered the submarine bay. The sub floated in the water, the gangway still connected. He crossed over it and entered the sub, moving to the controls to begin starting it up.

"Okay…" he whispered to himself. "Guess now all we've gotta do is wait for Erika to get here with the prisoners."

"For the record, I still think we're taking a big risk here."

"Noted, now how about we change the subject?" Silence lingered again and Masao rolled his eyes. "Oh come on, Himiko. Don't tell me you're going to pull the silent treatment crap on me."

"I'm not," she said and there was a noticeable shift in her tone. One that made Masao perk up and take notice.

"What's wrong?" he asked.

"I tried to bring Erika back into the channel, but… something's wrong. I've lost contact with her!"

CHAPTER 24

While Masao went to prepare the sub for departure, Erika had tasked herself with finding the sub's eventual passengers. She'd located the detention area and marked it on the map displayed on her AR-HUD.

Himiko's words still lingered in her head, though. Could she really hope to pull this off? To rescue these people without getting caught? She had already looped the camera footage, disabled the security alarms, and rerouted the guards away from the detention level. That would buy her some time, but she had no way of knowing if it would be enough.

But the effort had to be made nonetheless.

The detention level was one floor up from the sub's location. She made it there without a problem. There was a biometric scanner on the doors blocking access to the cells, but she'd already deactivated it from the control center and the door opened automatically once she stepped in front of it.

The room only contained one large cell that could safely house about a dozen prisoners. Except there were at least twice that presently housed inside. It was one thing to see it on a monitor, but seeing it right in front of her caused an even greater stir in the depths of Erika's soul.

The prisoners all looked at her with a mixture of fear and confusion on their faces. They didn't know who she was or what she was doing here, but they had no reason to expect anything other than the worst. Erika went to the cell door and drew her sword. The laser blade shimmered to life and there were gasps and even a few screams. Erika ignored them and sliced through the locking mechanism and the door swung open.

She retracted the sword and looked over their faces. Part of her wanted to show her face, to give them some sense that she was a person who was trying to help them. That would have been a mistake and she knew it. So she remained masked and spoke in English, the armor's built-in modulator distorting her voice.

"Don't be afraid. I'm going to get you all out of here."

"Wh-who *are* you?" one of them asked.

"The person who's going to save your life," she said. "But I can only do that if you follow me."

"And why should we trust you? They told us they were going to bring us here and give us work. Then they put us in here and every day, they take one person out. We never see them again."

Images flashed in Erika's mind of the man she'd fought back in Yoshiwara. Ignoring them was hard, but she had to stay focused.

"The way I see it, you have two choices. Either you can stay here and eventually get disappeared like the others," she said. "Or you can take your chances with me."

There were some murmurs among the group and hushed, whispered conversations. Some in English, some in other langauges Erika didn't recognize. Finally, a general sense of agreement rose from them.

"Good, now follow me," she said and led them through the door and down the hall. With a thought, her modulator was deactivated and she spoke so only those connected to her comm-link could hear. "I've got the refugees. How's the sub coming along?"

She tried to bring up the video feeds of both Himiko and Masao, but there was no link. Erika's armor attempted to establish a reconnection, but with no luck.

"If this is supposed to be a joke, it's not funny," she said.

"No, it's not a joke."

There was a new voice echoing in her head. Somehow, someone had tapped into her frequency and cut her off from her allies. The voice was disguised with a modulator and the image that was displayed on her AR-HUD was just static.

"Who is this?"

"I should ask you the same thing. When you interfaced with our systems, you gave us a path into your communications. Unfortunately, we haven't been able to get a visual on you or backtrace whoever it is you were speaking with. But no matter. Once you're dead, we can peel that armor off you and discover who you really are."

"I'd like to see you try," said Erika.

There was a distorted chuckle followed by, *"Famous last words."*

Erika's AR-HUD picked up on movement just around

the corner. She stopped and held out her hand in a gesture telling the refugees to halt their movements. The sword hilt slid into her hand and the energy blade flared to life again.

There was a lumbering noise. A creature turned the corner, an unholy amalgamation of technology and flesh. The skin was pulled tight over the face, half of which had been replaced by cybernetics. The right arm was still human, but the left had been replaced by a mechanical one that was so long, it would be dragging on the floor if the creature held it at his side. The monstrous arm ended in a hand with razor-sharp blades for fingers. The torso ended in mechanical hips and legs that put the poor soul at close to seven feet in height.

"Why are you doing this to them?" asked Erika.

"Because we're finding new weapons to use against the nation's enemies, new ways to improve our soldiers, and a method for these parasites to actually contribute to this great society of ours."

The cyborg let out an inhuman wail and swung his mechanical arm towards Erika. She rolled towards him, going under the arm. If she could get him further down the junction, she could clear a path for them to escape.

Erika sprung to her feet, activating the stun setting on her blade. The cyborg was hunched over and she was right within range. She jammed the sword into his chest, and he let out what sounded like a mix between a human scream and tearing metal.

When she pulled the sword from his chest, he lumbered back. His expression was fixed in its current form, so she couldn't get a sense of how he responded. But he did stand motionless, though she knew it wouldn't last long. However, she had managed to get him past the junction, leaving the corridor to the right open.

"Go," said Erika, glancing back over her shoulder. "Get to the stairs and go down to the bottom floor. Then find the submarine dock. I have a friend who will see that you get out of here safely."

Their expressions showed a mixture of emotions. Some clearly were worried of going off on their own, but others seemed to have concern for their savior. Others were still in a state of horror at the cybernetic creature that used to be one of them.

"Please, go now!" Erika ordered, louder this time. "I can't risk you getting hurt by this thing!"

That seemed to convince them to move and they started to flow towards the right down the corridor. She only hoped they could get down there before the security guards intercepted them. And she had to keep trying to connect to Masao or Himiko.

The cyborg stirred to life again, breaking out of his trance. His cybernetic eye, which glowed bright red, focused on Erika. The light it emanated became brighter, and Erika knew what was going to happen. She jumped as a laser fired from the eye, striking the spot where she had just stood and leaving a burn mark on the floor.

Once she caught her footing, she propelled herself at the creature's legs. She changed the setting to lethal, slicing through one of the legs and severing the knee. He collapsed, bracing himself on his cybernetic arm.

"A good strike, but it won't matter. Even if you can defeat my little pet, security will make certain your rescue attempt ends in tears."

He was right. She had to finish this off quickly and get down to the refugees. Erika jumped for the cybernetic arm, but instead of cutting it off, she used it as a springboard.

Her energy sword cut through the air and just as it was about to connect with his head, the eye unleashed another blast. This time, it struck her square in the chest and threw her against the wall.

Warnings flashed on Erika's AR-HUD, informing her of what the pain in her chest had already told her—the armor integrity had been compromised. She looked down and saw a hole right in her chest at the point where the blast struck. A scorch mark was on her bare skin and the nanites were struggling to slither in place and repair the damage.

"Dammit…" she muttered.

She got to her feet and readied her blade again, determined to press on even if her suit was compromised. Erika started moving again and the cyborg seemed to be preparing another blast from its eye. She raised the sword and it released an energy pulse that intercepted the cyborg's optic laser. Another pulse struck the cyborg's face and he reeled back.

The cyborg flailed, throwing his cybernetic arm around the area. Erika had to duck and dodge to avoid the blades. Her chest screamed in pain with every move she took, and she didn't know how much longer she could keep this going.

He recovered from the pulse and now swung at her with more coordination. Erika tried to flip away to avoid the latest strike, but the pain in her chest threw her off and she was slow to react. That allowed the cyborg to strike her with his claws.

Unlike the laser, the claws were not strong enough to pierce her armor. But his strength was enough to stagger her. She tried to shake it off when another blast hit her, this time striking her abdomen.

Erika dropped to her knees and hunched over. She had to brace herself on her hands to stop from faceplanting. More warnings flashed across the AR-HUD and the pain only got worse. She reached with a hand and felt the hole in her armor just below her ribcage.

"You can end this yourself, you know. Offer to stand down and I'll deactivate the cybernetics that are keeping him moving."

"And then what?" she asked.

"Then you will tell us just where you got your armor and who sent you."

"What about those people?"

A chuckle followed by, *"They **aren't** people. They're parasites."*

Erika raised her torso upright. She slid one leg forward, her knee bent and she leaned heavily on it as she pushed herself up. Her grip tightened around the tsuka and the blade flared to life once more.

"That's all I needed to hear," she said.

"Don't be an idiot. You can't win against him."

A new fire ignited in Erika. She pushed past the pain and rushed at the cyborg. The eye hummed once more and Erika deflected the blast with a pulse from her sword. She raised the energy sword and brought it down on the claws. The blade strained against them, having trouble going through the metal.

The cyborg tried to push against the sword. He fixed on Erika, his eye glowing again. She met his gaze and stayed determined, struggling against the claws while never looking away, timing her strike just right.

Then, she pulled away and the energy blade vanished. The force the cyberg had been using to fight against the blade now had no more resistance and his arm flew up just as the eye unleashed another optic beam. The laser ended up blowing a hole right through the cybernetic hand.

The cyborg recoiled in pain and Erika used this as her chance. She maneuvered around the flailing arm and jumped on his back, then jammed the energy blade into the spot where his head met his neck.

The scream was cut short and the cyborg collapsed. Erika fell on the ground herself and remained there for a moment. She was eye-level with the cyborg and she watched as the red light in its cybernetic eye slowly dimmed to blackness.

"What have you done?"

"Put that poor soul out of his misery," she said, just as footsteps echoed through the hall. Erika's AR-HUD warned her of approaching figures, as if she couldn't tell herself. She pulled herself up in time to meet the barrels of a dozen assault rifles all trained on her.

CHAPTER 25

Erika's armor had been breached and now she found herself staring down the barrels of a dozen assault rifles. She wondered if the armor was still strong enough to hold up to them, or if she even had the energy to keep on fighting. But as she tightened her grip on the tsuka, she knew she was determined to try.

"You've put up a good fight, my friend. But now, the best thing for you to do is to stand down. I'd hate to have to kill someone who has proven so capable in battle."

"Go to hell," was her response as she strained to rise to her feet.

The guards tracked her with their weapons. She saw that their fingers had moved inside the trigger guards. At the slightest provocation, they would fire on her. If this was the end, then at least she'd go out fighting.

"YAH!"

The shout came from behind. The guards blocked her view and they all turned to the source. They opened fire and while they were distracted, Erika took her opportunity. She activated her blade and rammed it through the back of the guard closest to her.

Another turned his attention to her and she was thankfully within range enough to slice through his barrel and she performed an elbow-strike on his face.

There were other groans and screams of pain from further ahead. As the guards fell before her and the other mysterious attacker, her view became unobstructed. And what she saw was Masao cutting through them one by one.

He moved faster than she expected, and judging from the pristine state of his armor, seemed he hadn't encountered any resistance until now. Erika took a few steps back to just watch the battle unfold. The guards were certainly no match for him alone, so it gave her the chance to run a check on her armor systems.

"Two of you, huh? That won't do. If you think you're going to escape from here, you're sadly mistaken."

"Judging from how we've taken out your guards, seems you won't have much of a say in that," said Erika.

"We'll see about that."

The line went dead. Erika wasn't sure what he meant, but she knew she didn't like the tone. There were just a few guards still standing. Even though her armor wasn't in the best state—or herself, for that matter—she needed to help Masao to speed things up.

Masao weaved between the guards, dodging and deflecting gunfire. He alternated between sword slashes, kicks, and elbow strikes. Even a headbutt or two. Erika came in from the rear. While Masao drew their fire, she attacked from behind and cut them down.

Her movements were sluggish compared to normal and

every single action she took sent pain ringing through her body. As she cringed after a kick, she suddenly felt another sensation—that of something warm and wet on her side.

Erika's eyes shot downward and she saw a guard pulling a dagger from her abdomen. He had stabbed her in the spot where her armor had been compromised. She hadn't felt it going in, but now that it was out, she felt a dull throb that began to increase in its intensity.

"No!"

The voice was Masao's, but he sounded distant. Everything seemed to move in slow-motion. Erika looked from her bloodstained hand up to the guard as he raised his gun to eye-level with her. He squeezed the trigger and there was a burst of light, then the feeling of the bullet striking her helmet.

Erika's head rocked back and that impact drew her out of her shock. Time returned to normal just as she saw Masao grab the gun. He turned it on the guard and fired several times right in his chest. Masao dropped the gun and then focused on Erika.

"Hey! You okay in there? Can you hear me?"

Erika tried to shake off the effects of shock, but the pain had now become piercing. "Bastard stabbed me…"

"Yeah, so I see," he said. "You okay to move?"

"I'm fine, just—" she cringed again as she tried to move, "—takes some effort."

Masao knelt down and examined the wound. He placed his hand on it and some of the nanites from his armor flowed onto her, covering the wound and applying pressure.

"Himiko said she lost contact with you, so I went to see what the deal was. Along the way, I found your people and got them on the sub," said Masao.

"Good," she said. "We have to get out of here now. Whoever's in charge of this facility was able to disrupt my comm and speak with me directly. He gave some sort of vague threat and then just vanished. I think they might be planning something."

"In other words, we probably shouldn't linger around here." Masao picked up one of the discarded guns. "Can you shoot?"

She nodded and took the gun in her right hand. Masao put her left arm around his shoulders and supported her as they went down the hall towards the stairwell. Going down was a bit difficult with her wounds, but she managed to do it thanks to Masao's aid. And when they reached the bottom level, the door opened with two guards standing and waiting.

Erika raised the gun and squeezed the trigger, spraying them both and taking them out of the equation. Masao pulled her along with him, trying to increase the pace. It sent more pain through her body, but she did as best she could.

They managed to get to the submarine dock without too much trouble. The fact that they faced so little resistance caused Erika worry over what exactly her mysterious adversary had planned. And as if on cue, that's when the rumbling began.

The entire complex shuddered and shook. Masao stumbled and Erika fell from his grip, hitting the floor. He helped pull her back to her feet as he struggled to keep from staggering himself.

"Shit, what's going on?" asked Masao.

A pit formed in Erika's stomach. "I think they're destroying the facility…"

"Fuck!"

"C'mon, we have to hurry!" said Erika as she tried to move towards the gangway.

Masao kept his grip on her and pulled her along with her. As they continued on their path, the complex shook again. A rafter right overhead fell. Masao pushed her away just seconds before it crashed down.

Erika landed on her hands, gritting her teeth in pain. She pushed herself onto her back and strained to sit up. The fallen rafter was just ahead and Masao was pinned beneath it. She moved forward, crawling forward to him, even as the quakes continued—growing more frequent.

"What are you doing, Kuroki?" he asked. "Get your ass to the sub already!"

"You came back for me and I'll be damned if I don't return the favor."

She got to her feet and crouched low, wrapping her hands around the bars of the rafter. Erika strained to try and lift the rafter off him. After a few moments of trying, she relented and took a breath, then glanced down at Masao.

"Are you going to help or what?" she asked.

"Just go!"

"Shut up and push."

Erika gripped the rafter again and again tried to pull it off. This time, Masao contributed effort, trying to push up against the rafter. It started to move and he could slide one leg out and bent the knee. Erika's legs straightened just a little more and Masao was able to free himself from the rafter.

"You can still walk?" she asked.

He nodded and stood, then put his arm around Erika's waist and they went for the gangplank. They quickly crossed and boarded the submarine. While Masao went to the controls, Erika checked on the refugees she'd spared. Seemed everyone had made it onboard in one piece.

"What happened?" asked one of them. "That…thing?"

"It's over," said Erika. "You're going to be okay now."

"Everyone hold onto something, gonna get a bit bumpy!" Masao shouted from the front.

The submarine descended and Masao opened the door via remote controls in the cockpit. It rocketed out from the complex just as the ceiling came down behind them.

Erika checked the periscope and looked back at the island. Explosions blasted out from various points of the extinct volcano, which would no doubt draw attention from the mainland. She lowered the periscope and joined Masao in the cockpit, taking the seat beside him.

"What now?" she asked.

"Himiko says Miyata has a place we can take them," said Masao. "We're heading there now, then we have to destroy the sub and see about getting you some medical attention."

"You sure they're not tracking us in this thing?"

"No. Which is why we have to ditch it sooner rather than later," said Masao. "But hopefully blowing that facility will have slowed them down from responding."

Erika rested her head against the rear of her chair. That's when the voice returned.

"You may think you've one, but you haven't. I'll find out who you and your friend are. Eventually."

"We'll see about that," said Erika before cutting off all communications with her armor.

CHAPTER 26

Days had passed since Erika and Masao's liberation of the Hachijo-Kojima facility. In that time, Erika and Masao had mostly stuck to casual pleasantries throughout their workday as she attempted to keep up the ruse of investigating leads into Miyata's disappearance. Naturally, none of them panned out, which was her intention.

Then one day, Erika felt a presence behind her while working at her terminal. She spun her chair around and saw Hiro standing there, looking down at her.

"Do you have a minute?" he asked.

"Sure," she said and then stood from her desk.

Hiro led her from their section office and over to the elevator. He hit the call button and folded his arms, waiting in silence. As Erika waited by his side, her mind kept throwing possibilities in front of her.

Did he know something about her involvement? Did that guy at the facility who had co-opted her comm somehow manage to identify her? Was he after answers about the Miyata investigation? Or what if Miyata hadn't been as skilled in co-opting the armor as he had believed and Hiro discovered where her and Masao went?

The elevator arrived and they both stepped inside. Hiro asked for the executive level and Erika's fears grew. That could only mean that they were going up to speak to the general. She still recalled her one and only meeting with Hojo at the welcome party and how uncomfortable he'd made her feel.

She decided to finally take a chance and speak first. "Where are we going?"

"General Hojo would like an update about the Miyata investigation," said Hiro.

Just as she feared.

"Is that common?" she asked.

"No," said Hiro. "But it's his prerogative. And this is a pretty sensitive issue given Yoshida's relationship with the government."

"It's strange to hear you talk about your family's company as if you're completely disconnected."

She felt his eyes boring into her. With a hint of sheepishness, she met his gaze and then looked down.

"Sorry. It's not my place."

"Kuroki, I want you to know something about me," said Hiro. "I'm not my family nor my company. My father actually couldn't have been angrier when I told him I was going into military service. He wanted to groom me as his successor but I felt I had a duty to serve the state."

"Again, sorry," said Erika.

"Don't apologize," said Hiro. "I just want you to know that I'm not here because of my father's connections. I got to where I am all on my own."

The elevator slowed to a stop and the doors opened. Hiro emerged first and led her down the hall towards the double-doors with the characters for Hojo's name on a plaque just to the side of them. He pushed the button below the plaque and the doors slid open.

The office was fairly spacious with a small seating area. Two leather chairs on either side of a low table. The large window gave a view of the Tokyo skyline. Portraits were mounted on the walls of various military and political leaders.

The desk's size matched the room. The high-backed executive chair was turned towards the window, and a haze of smoke hung in the air. The chair turned and she saw the aged face of General Hojo, a cigarette clamped in the lips beneath his silver mustache.

Hiro bowed once Hojo turned to face them and Erika followed suit. Hojo remained still, his hard eyes taking in Erika. That same uncomfortable feeling from the welcome party had returned in full force.

"Agent Kuroki," said Hojo, addressing her as if it were the first time he'd ever spoken to her. "Agent Yoshida tells me you've been investigating the disappearance of Kenjiro Miyata, correct?"

"Yessir," she said.

"Please inform me of what you've learned."

Erika cleared her throat. She'd rehearsed this several times, but she never expected to give the update to Hojo personally. Her heart was pounding and it felt like her stomach was about to drop.

"Unfortunately, I haven't learned much," she said. "When Agent Yoshida tasked me with this mission, I began by consulting with cyberterrorism to identify his tracer. But he had somehow managed to disable it, and Section Chief Adachi suggested the possibility of black market implants. I also investigated Miyata's last-known residence, where I found photographs of a woman named Keiko Izumi and two foreign-born girls. Yet records show Izumi is dead and as of yet we've found no information on the children."

Hojo drew on his cigarette, the embers glowing bright as they consumed more of the rolled paper. He took the cigarette from his mouth and clouds of smoke were propelled through his nostrils.

"Did you consult with Yoshida Technologies?"

She nodded. "I did. I visited their main office in Shibuya and spoke with Gardner Takasu. He was able to provide me with redacted files regarding projects Miyata had worked on, but had no further information for me."

"And in those files?"

Erika shook her head. "I'm still working through them, but as of yet, I haven't found anything noteworthy."

"I see," said Hojo. "What of the two who attacked you and this drive they were seeking?"

"I have suspicions Miyata may have hired them, but he did everything through encrypted channels. I attempted to set up a rendezvous, yet unfortunately he never showed."

Hojo's eyes moved from Erika and now targeted Hiro. "Agent Yoshida, is there anything you have to add?"

Yoshida stood still, hands grasped behind his back. He shook his head and said, "I have reviewed all of Agent Kuroki's progress reports. She's been operating as efficiently as possible but I believe Miyata is simply too good at what he does to be found."

"So it would seem," said Hojo. "Quite a pity, I'm afraid. Not only losing a man of his skill, but the information he possesses could make him a very dangerous man."

"Sir, I'm more than willing to continue the search if that is what the General wishes," Erika added.

Hojo took the cigarette from his lips again and waved the hand dismissively, leaving wisps of smoke trails in his wake.

"No, I don't think that will be necessary. Thank you for your report, Agent Kuroki. Please return to your station, you are dismissed."

Erika bowed and glanced at Hiro, who did the same. But as they both turned to leave, Hojo called out once more.

"Agent Yoshida, just a moment, if you don't mind," he said. "I would like to discuss something with you."

Hiro nodded for Erika to go on ahead and then turned to once more face the general. Erika left the office and made her way back to the elvator alone. While waiting for the elevator, she wondered what exactly it could be that the general wished to discuss with Hiro. It seemed she was out of the woods for now, but they could have been trying to trap her.

This was what Masao dealt with every single day. She wondered just how he did it.

浪人

The rest of the day fortunately passed without incident. Hiro had eventually returned from his private meeting with Hojo, though he said nothing of what they discussed. His demeanor was completely normal when he returned, so Erika believed herself to be in the clear for the time being.

Later, after she returned home, she received an encrypted message asking her to return to Himiko's place. Erika had waited until midnight just as she had the first time, then made the trek out to Roppongi under the cover of night.

When she arrived, she found Himiko standing behind the bar and Masao sat on a stool in front of it. The two old friends were sharing a drink and laughing together. Erika slowly approached them, and after they finished their conversation, they finally acknowledged her presence.

"What's going on?" asked Erika. "What happened to the people?"

"The people are quite all right, Agent Kuroki." That fourth voice came from the darkness in the former club. Miyata emerged from the shadows, with a warm smile on his face. "Thanks to you, that is."

"Don't thank me too much. I wasn't able to save that guy they butchered," said Erika.

"No one could have. He was too far gone," said Miyata.

"What will happen to the ones we got out?" asked Erika.

"Our people are setting them up with forged identities, tryin' to get them into the system," said Himiko. "It'll take time, but there are some communities we can get them into. They won't all be together, but they'll be alive."

"It's all 'cause of you, Kuroki," said Masao. "I don't know if I would've had the will to go against Himiko if not for what you said. I might've just stuck with the mission."

"Don't think I'm not still pissed at both of you for that," said Himiko before taking a sip of her drink. "But you did good nonetheless."

"And what about the mission? Did you get what you needed?" asked Erika.

"Yeah, we got it," said Himiko. "We're flooding social

media. The government's censorbots are working overtime trying to take it down, but so far we're staying a step ahead."

"That's something, I suppose," said Erika. She was glad the mission was a success and that those people would manage to have some kind of a life after all this. Though her thoughts still lingered on that cyborg she had to kill.

"You don't seem too happy," said Masao. "Want a drink?"

Erika sighed and shook her head. "I just can't stop thinking about that guy."

"It's tragic, I know," said Miyata. "Though I suspect he won't be the last we run across."

"Why is Yoshida doing all this?" asked Erika. "A process like that wouldn't do the Tokkei any good."

"Tokkei's just one division. You guys aren't who they're worried about," said Himiko. "They're thinkin' bigger than that."

"That's what I'm afraid of," said Miyata. "An underclass of people without a voice or any advocates. Butchered and maimed. They're strong and they can be controlled, used in overseas conflicts."

"That's what you think the government is up to?" asked Erika.

"I believe so," said Miyata. "The work we do here, it's just one cog in a larger machine. A resistance. But we can't do it alone. Even with Masao's help, I'm afraid it won't be enough."

"You're asking me to join up with you, aren't you?" asked Erika.

"We could do a lot of good with you on our side," said Miyata. "Take a real stand against the government."

Erika sighed. "I don't think that's possible. I helped you

out, but I don't think I can be part of this."

"Those people weren't the only ones in danger," said Himiko. "You heard what he said, Yoshida's not going to stop."

"I know," said Erika. "But we stopped just one machine, and it will probably start up again. How can we fight against something that powerful? Odds that impossible?"

Miyata went over to the bar and sat on the stool. He took a breath before speaking, not addressing anyone in particular. "Do you know the story of *The Forty-Seven Ronin*?"

"They made us read it in the Jietai," said Erika. "It's a story about honor and devotion to one's master."

"Yes, that's true. Though I think there's another message in the story, one that's often overlooked by those who use it to encourage unflinching loyalty to the government," said Miyata. "The court official, Kira, was corrupt and felt that the daimyo, Asano, would not offer him the bribes he wanted. After numerous offenses, Asano had reached his limit and attacked Kira. He failed to kill Kira and was sentenced to commit *seppuku*.

"After his ritual suicide, Asano's lands and possessions were confiscated by the government, his family was to be left ruined, and his retainers would become masterless. Of the over three hundred men Asano had commanded, forty-seven refused to allow Kira's deeds to go unpunished. Even though revenge had been prohibited by the shogunate, they still pursued justice.

"So while the military may use this story to teach about loyalty, I see something different in it," Miyata concluded. "I see this as a story of heroes seeking justice against corrupt leadership. In fact, I see it as a statement that it is our duty to fight for justice in such instances."

Erika thought about the story Miyata had told. Of all the times she had been made to read accounts of *The Forty-Seven Ronin*, she had never viewed it in that light. Indeed, she doubted few had ever seen it the way Miyata had. And his rendition made a compelling case.

"The ronin in the story," she began, "in the end, they turned themselves in and were sentenced to death."

"I'm not saying it's a perfect comparison," said Miyata. "But it gives you something to think about. When faced with the sinister acts of our leaders, can we really just stand by and do nothing?"

"So we'd become modern-day *ronin*, eh?" asked Masao. "I gotta admit, Erika, I kinda like the sound of that."

"There is a lot of good the four of us can do together," said Miyata. "What do you say, Agent Kuroki? Are you ready to make a difference in this world?"

"I..." Erika paused.

Everything he told her made so much sense. And she wondered if she could truly just go back to being a simple Tokkei agent after what she'd witnessed. Ultimately, she had to reach the conclusion that such a thing was not possible.

"When do we start?" she asked.

EPILOGUE

General Hojo stood in the open-air section of the Andaz Rooftop Bar in Toranomon. He held a glass of shochu in one hand and a cigar in the other, alternating between the two as he waited for his guest. While he waited, he admired the view of Tokyo from this vantage.

He didn't like the notion of meeting with his contact tonight. Hojo didn't trust the man as far as he could throw him. But the company trusted him and as a result, Hojo had no choice other than to play nice. So when he heard the man's slightly accented Japanese greeting, he tried his best to hide his contempt.

"Good evening, General. Thank you for meeting me tonight." Gardner Takasu had a good command of the language and he was properly respectful and deferential, but it wasn't enough for Hojo.

"Mr. Takasu," said the general before puffing on the cigar. "I appreciate everything you've done for us, but I have to question just exactly why you wanted to meet in the open like this."

"If you came to my office or I to yours, there would be logs of our meeting," said Gardner. "Here, however, no one is keeping any logs."

"And it's public, so if I don't like what you have to say, I couldn't kill you," said Hojo. "That's your real calculation, isn't it?"

Gardner's plastic smile remained fixed on his face. Instead of addressing Hojo's question, he continued on with business.

"The reason I wanted to meet is because of the attack on the Hachijo facility."

"Have you found out who the culprit was?"

"We have an image." Gardner reached inside his suit jacket and took a physical photograph. The image was a person clad in armor reminiscent of that worn by Tokkei agents in the field—however the color was different. "I was able to break in on their frequency, but the voice was disguised so I couldn't tell who it was. All I know is that whoever the pilot of this armor is, they're quite good at their job. They dispatched one of our cyborgs."

Hojo examined the photograph and then returned it to Gardner. "What are you telling me, Takasu? That this whole thing is *my* fault?"

"It certainly seems like Tokkei armor, doesn't it?"

"Armor manufactured by *your* company. And correct me if I'm wrong, but wasn't Kenjiro Miyata the architect of that armor?"

Gardner's lips tightened. Hojo had made him uncomfortable and that pleased the old general. He took a sip from his shochu while maintaining a fixed gaze on the foreign-born executive.

"Perhaps the real issue here is you," said Hojo. "After all, you're not truly one of us, are you? You can speak our language, you know our customs, and maybe you have Old Man Yoshida fooled, but nothing changes what you really are. One could argue that you have more sympathy for those wretches than with our mission."

Gardner held his tongue for some time after Hojo finished his rant. He took a deep breath before he answered the general's thinly veiled accusations.

"I understand your anger, General. Your suspicions are not unwarranted. However, I should remind you that despite my birthplace, I was raised here. I have worked hard my entire life to get to where I am. And I have proven my dedication to our mission. I have no sympathy for those invaders, that I can promise you. And as this program falls under my purview, I am the one who will end up on the chopping block should it go south. So I would appreciate the benefit of the doubt."

Hojo hated the young man, but he couldn't deny that he managed to make a convincing argument. He finished the shochu, leaving the ice clinking in the glass and took a few more puffs on the cigar before he continued.

"Very well," said Hojo. "So perhaps you can tell me what your suspicions are? Is this a Tokkei agent or just someone wearing a suit?"

"Truthfully, we don't know at the moment," said Gardner. "The data we obtained from the cyborg before the facility was destroyed was corrupted and we're trying to piece it back together. The suits are equipped with sophisticated failsafes, so if it were countermanded, that would take quite a bit of effort."

"So would building a replica, correct?"

"In theory, yes. Unless someone had the resources to do so," said Gardner. "Regardless of what the truth is, I think we can both be certain that Miyata is involved. This happening so soon after his disappearance seems far too coincidental, wouldn't you agree?"

"You're right," said Hojo. "But we haven't managed to find him. His disappearing act was planned for some time and he managed to pull it off right under all our noses."

"I suggest keeping a watchful eye on your people. We don't know if one of them is involved with Miyata, but we can't rule out the possibility."

"What about the son?" asked Hojo. "He's never been on the best of terms with his father."

"Hiro Yoshida is certainly someone who should be closely watched," said Gardner. "You're absolutely right, we can't rule him out. But we also can't risk accusing him of anything without evidence. Despite their chilly relationship, the old man still hopes his son will return to the fold. And if we do anything to jeopardize that without having anything solid, it would mean both our heads."

"I'll see what my people can find," said Hojo. "What about your part?"

Gardner smiled. "Our engineers are already hard at work at something. Something that I believe will be a game-changer and might just mean the end of this interloper."

AFTER WORD

The story of Ronin's creation was an interesting one that dates back several years. I was in my third year living in Japan and beginning to study Japanese history, in particular the postwar era. I was also getting pretty heavily involved in the New Pulp movement at that time, and I started thinking about potential new characters.

One day, this idea hit me—a lot of the classic pulp characters debuted and were featured in a time period of intense economic anxiety, namely the Great Depression. And postwar Japan was also a time of great economic anxiety, plus had the added benefit of a country on the verge of massive change, an occupying military force, and the rise of criminal elements and the black market. Plus there were also things to pull from real life, such as secret societies (the Black Dragon Society) and mad scientists (Shiro Ishii and Unit 731).

My idea was a former Japanese soldier who felt betrayed by his country and gains possession of an ancient, mystic sword created by the famed swordsmith, Muramasa. But as with many ideas I've had over the years, it just never materialized and I ended up getting caught up in other projects.

Eventually though, those other projects had come to their conclusions. After my attempts at a Japanese detective series didn't pan out, I had this urge to write some additional books in Japan.

As luck would have it, I was asked by my school if I wanted to teach a class in Japanese cinema. Since Japanese cinema is why I had a desire to come to Japan in the first place, I jumped at the chance. And one of the movies I chose to cover was Kinji Fukasaku's 2000 classic, *Battle Royale*.

The last time I saw *Battle Royale* was actually before I moved to Japan over ten years ago. Obviously since that time, I'd learned a lot about Japanese history, society, and politics. And when I rewatched the movie to prepare for the class, I was absolutely amazed. This movie had so much going on in it that I'd never noticed before.

Watching and discussing that movie with my students started giving me ideas about a futuristic Japan extrapolated from what has been happening in the present. With Japan's declining population, there are a lot of conversations about opening up immigration. At the same time, the ruling political party is very xenophobic and the prime minister has pushed for unnerving policies including undermining Japan's pacifist constitution and expanding state secrecy laws in order to silence the press. With his connections to an ultra-nationalist cult and his admiration for his grandfather (a former prime minister as well as a fascist war criminal who despised democracy), I wondered about what that world would look like.

That's what led to the creation of this world. I had also felt an itch to do a superhero book again after my *Vanguard* series was completed back in 2016. So this felt like the perfect storm of elements in order to bring this world to life. As I was trying to think of a name for Erika's costumed identity, I realized that the name Ronin, which I would have used for my postwar pulp hero, would actually fit very well. Especially when I thought of the story of *The 47 Ronin*. And when you also factor in Masao's presence (who ended up inserting himself into the action without my permission), the term Ronin actually applies to both these characters as opposed to just one.

This was a fun world to create and a fun book to write. I'm hoping there will be more books in this series. And if you share that hope, I'd like to ask that you do your part in supporting this book by leaving a review on Amazon and recommending it to other people who might enjoy it.

Thanks so much for reading, and I'll see you in the next book!

Perry Constantine
May 2020
Kagoshima, Japan

ABOUT THE AUTHOR

Born and raised in the Chicagoland area, Percival Constantine grew up on a fairly consistent diet of superhero comics, action movies, video games, and TV shows. At the age of ten, he first began writing and has never really stopped.

Percival has been working in publishing since 2005 in various capacities—author, editor, formatter, letterer—and has written books, short stories, comics, and more. He has a Bachelor of Arts in English and Mass Media from Northeastern Illinois University and a Master of Arts in English and Screenwriting from Southern New Hampshire University. He currently resides in southern Japan, where he teaches literature and film while continuing to write.